BEAR KILL!

Marcus Quinn and his Raiders ran ahead to find a huge black bear reared up, clawing at the Cheyenne hunter. Five other braves followed, bows and arrows ready.

"Shoot him!" Billy Joe shouted, lifting his rifle.

"No!" Quinn ordered. "Indian's too close!"

Bob Depro gave a loud roar, distracting the animal long enough for the trapped Cheyenne to escape. As the bear lifted its head, Depro shot him in the head with his pistol.

The bear hardly noticed it.

Then five arrows flew, piercing the bear's chest and front legs. It bellowed in rage but kept on coming.

Loomis Depro, his nine-and-a-half-inch Bowie knife drawn, powered in from behind, leaped on the big animal's back, and drove the sharp blade in its thick throat. He stabbed again and again, ripping out more fur and flesh each time. The bear roared and reached up with its claws, trying to knock Loomis off.

Suddenly, a gout of blood surged out the beast's throat and it dropped to all fours. Loomis vaulted clear. The Cheyenne hunters sent another five arrows into the weakened bear. Eyes glazed over, the seven-hundred-pound bear shook its shaggy head, fell on its side, shivered once, then lay still in a growing pool of hot red blood.

The QUINN'S RAIDERS series:

QUINN'S RAIDERS

RED BLUFF REVENGE

J. D. Bodine

LYNX BOOKS
New York

Special thanks to Chet Cunningham

QUINN'S RAIDERS: RED BLUFF REVENGE

ISBN: 1-55802-040-3

First Printing/June 1989

This is a work of fiction. Names, characters, places, and incidents are either the product of the author's imagination or are used fictitiously. Any resemblance to actual events, locales, or persons, living or dead, is entirely coincidental.

This book is published by Lynx Books, a division of Lynx Communications, Inc., 41 Madison Avenue, New York, New York, 10010. The name "Lynx" and the logo consisting of a stylized head of a lynx are trademarks of Lynx Communications, Inc.

Printed in the United States of America

0 9 8 7 6 5 4 3 2 1

QUINN'S RAIDERS

RED BLUFF REVENGE

THE SNARLING SHOT of a high-powered rifle shattered the dark silence in the high country near Red Bluff, Wyoming. The heavy bullet jolted into the stagecoach driver. He had been pushing his rig north from the border of Colorado toward Red Bluff.

The driver slammed off the coach seat and vanished in the darkness over the side of the coach. The twelve reins dropped slack over the backs of the six-horse team. The suddenly unattended animals charged ahead for a moment in panic, then slowed as two wheels rolled into a shallow ditch at the side of the trail and came to a stop.

From each side of the coach, figures charged up on horses, caught the team of six, and held them. Two pistol shots shattered the sudden silence at the seven-thousand-foot level of the Medicine Bow Mountain foothills.

"Out!" a voice bellowed. In the darkness two women, a drummer, and one small girl stepped down from the coach. They looked around, trembling as the riders came closer. The four riders had no saddles, they wore Indian feathered headdresses, and each carried a bow across his back.

1

All had revolvers as well.

"Indians!" one of the women whispered. The other passengers pretended not to hear. They were shaking so badly they could hardly stand.

"Lay on ground!" the same man's guttural voice commanded. The women hesitated, but the window-glass salesman who was sweating and shivering at the sight of the savages went down at once. He had never been this close to the heathen savages before in his life. The women followed his example and stretched out on the stage road. Mrs. H. Wilson Carmichael was the last. She held her four-year-old daughter, Kitty, close to her side as she lay down on her stomach in the dust.

Suddenly one of the men who had dismounted grabbed Kitty and tore her from Mrs. Carmichael's hands. She could barely see him in the darkness.

"No, no, not my baby!" Mrs. Carmichael screamed. A revolver fired and the slug passed close to the screaming woman. The savage handed the girl to a mounted brave, then leaped onto his own horse, and all four fired their revolvers into the air before they rode away into the night. One rider slowed and turned.

The drummer lifted himself up and stared at the retreating savages. Two revolver shots crashed into the Wyoming dark stillness. One hit the drummer in the head, and he slammed backward, dead in an instant.

The man who fired the shot wheeled his mount and galloped after the three others who rode down the stage road in the direction of Red Bluff. They kept to the road for a mile, then turned off to the west into the foothills and stopped beside a huge cottonwood next to a small creek.

They joked about the holdup, guffawed about the Indian headdresses they wore. One by one they

2

heaved saddles on the horses and cinched them up, then they remounted in the more familiar saddles and hurried away. They made good time.

Two miles off the road they slowed and walked their mounts. Three of them pulled off the feathered Indian headdresses and draped them over their horses' necks.

"Christ, but I'm glad to get out of that damn thing," Slade said. He was tall and slender, had been a sergeant in the Union army in the big war before he decided he'd had enough of being shot at, and deserted. He held the small girl with one arm around her middle and pinned her to his torso.

"Hey, Slade, think we fooled them?" the man beside him asked. His name was Dirk and he was short and fat.

"Damn right, we fooled them," Possum said. "Just them three scared women left. They see feathers and they think injun right away. No doubt they'll say we is Indians, sure as shit!" Possum, a country boy from Illinois, had arms that hung almost to his knees.

"What do you think, Flinch?" Slade asked the fourth rider.

"Goddamn, you see me nail that jasper?" Flinch asked. "I got that little bastard with a fucking head shot from near to fifty feet away! Christ, what a good shot!" Flinch was of medium height, gaunt to the point of sickness, with sunken cheeks, dark eyes deep in their sockets, and was almost bald under his battered low-crowned dirty brown hat.

"Flinch, stop patting yourself on the butt and answer the question," Slade said. "Did we fool them women into thinking we was Cheyenne Indians?"

"Hell yes, we fooled them. I even feel like a sneaky, scalping Indian. That's what I should have done, scalped the jehu!"

Dirk took out his knife in the pale moonlight and

touched the blade to his thumb. "Yeah, why didn't I think of that before? Always wanted to try to lift somebody's hair. What a good chance I missed."

"No goddamned scalping!" Slade bellowed. "Told you before. My granddaddy got scalped and I never seen such a damned thing in my life. His brains was sticking right out of his head. He lived for two days after it, and I never want to see that again. No scalping!"

Possum looked over at their leader. "Yeah, okay, Slade. We understand. You think this little trick will get the Army after the damn Cheyenne?"

"Better. If it don't, we wasted a lot of time."

"I want my mama!" a small voice screamed.

"Well, so the kid can talk," Slade said. He held her tighter. "You don't get your mama for a long time, now keep quiet or I'll make you walk."

Four-year-old Kitty Carmichael started crying. She screamed in terror for a moment, then settled down to crying like her heart was breaking.

"Can't you shut up the kid, Slade?" Flinch asked. "Hey, any damn reason we got to keep her alive?"

"Yeah, a damn good one. We ain't just snatching her. After the cavalry rides in and cleans out them Cheyenne off the Little Laramie River, then we send a ransom note to old H. Wilson Carmichael. We collect on both ends here!"

Dirk laughed. "Slade, you're really a rotten son of a bitch, you know that?"

"Damn right, and I'm getting worse every day!"

All four of them laughed and kept riding. Kitty at last gave up her crying. She was only four years old but practical. If crying didn't bring results, she would try something else. She just hadn't figured out what to do yet.

The four men rode for another three hours, and at

last came to a small cabin hidden in a copse of aspen and cottonwood. The cabin was twelve feet square and built solidly of ponderosa pine logs. The men guessed the place had been put up by some mountain man trapper forty years before.

He had hidden it in the trees so the Indians wouldn't find it. Evidently they hadn't, since it didn't get burned down. It was one large room, with a fireplace opposite the one door.

The four riders put their horses in a pole corral concealed behind the cabin. When Slade pushed the door open his six-gun was out, but no one was there. Everything was as they had left it. A fire had been laid in the fireplace before they left, and now Slade lit it.

"Possum, get us some grub ready," Slade called. "Been riding all damn day and I'm hungry."

Slade sat on one of the bunks and surveyed his team. Not much of an army, not even a gang, but it was all he had. He had chanced on the Little Laramie River two months ago and with his gold pan had come out with over two ounces of gold in one afternoon.

He knew the Cheyenne were camped less than a mile away and had hunters through that area all the time. But he took a chance and panned that one stretch of water. He'd do anything to get back there. But he didn't want to wind up as his grandfather had—his hair decorating some Indian lance.

So, he had to get rid of the Cheyenne. Best way was to have the Army do the job. He spent a week in Laramie, learning what was going on, who was important, how the local politics worked, how strong the Army post was nearby.

The newspaper said that Mrs. Carmichael and her daughter would be returning from visiting relatives near the Colorado border. They would come in from the southwest on the Mountain Stage Lines. He knew by then that Carmichael was the guy who owned the big gold mine up in the Medicine Bows. If the Cheyenne were charged with child stealing—and the kid would be on a stage in an out-of-the way area—it wouldn't be hard to work out a plan.

Slade needed three other men to pull off the stunt, and he found them in the Red Bluff saloons. Gold fever was rampant in the town right then, and any hint of a new strike or a panning operation would bring a rawhide army of panners.

He had been careful, selective, and picked out three men who would do anything for a good mining strike. He bought them drinks, explained the operation, and formed his squad.

Slade went to where the small girl sat on the bunk next to the fire.

"Kitty, we're not going to hurt you. We want to be your friends. We'll talk with your daddy about taking you home. Until then, you'll be staying with us here."

"No! I want my mama!"

Slade automatically moved his hand but stopped it before he slapped her. He controlled his temper and shook his head.

"No, Kitty. You'll be staying with us. If you be good, we'll let you wander around the cabin. If you're not good, we'll tie you up to a bunk. You understand?"

Kitty promptly began to cry and kicked the bed and flailed it with both hands.

Slade watched her and for just a fraction of a second wondered if this had been a good idea. Then he knew it had. There was nothing like a kidnapping to get people aroused, to get a family worked up. It also should put a lot of pressure on the military, and the Fort Sanders commander.

Slade grinned at his three men. "Hey, don't worry, everything is going fine. In a week, at the most, the

Army will move in and drive the Cheyenne out of the Little Laramie River and we'll be in there panning gold like you've never seen. Want to see the poke I brought out in about three hours?"

It had taken him all day to pan the two ounces, but they didn't have to know that. Just seeing the yellow dust would be plenty to reenthuse these three pawns of his. Gold fever was one disease that there was only one cure for—finding real gold. He had them hooked.

"My baby! My baby! Bring back my baby!" Mrs. Carmichael screamed the words over and over as the four figures rode away into the night. She stood and raced after them down the rough stage road. Ten yards along, she tripped and sprawled in the dirt, slamming on her chest and hands, digging up the dirt that sprayed into her face and dress.

She sat up wailing. "Bring back my Kitty!"

One of the other women on the stage hurried up to Mrs. Carmichael and comforted her.

"There, there, now, Mrs. Carmichael. Kitty is gone. What we have to do now is concentrate on getting back to town to get help."

Mrs. Carmichael continued to wail. Tears streamed down her cheeks and dripped off her chin.

"Bring back my baby Kitty," she said again, softly this time, almost a prayer.

"We'll do our best to find her, Mrs. Carmichael," Martha Turner said. "Right now I need you to help me get the stage back on the road. The driver is dead; so is that salesman. Now, are you going to help us or just sit there and cry?"

Mrs. Carmichael sat up straighter. She slashed at the tears on her cheeks. It had to be done. First they had to get to Red Bluff.

"Yes, I'll help. What can I do?"

"Have you ever driven a team of six?"

"No, but I have driven four. I think I can do it." They walked back to the team. The horses had stopped twenty yards down the road but the stage sat only half on the roadway, with two wheels in a shallow ditch.

"What about the bodies?" Mrs. Carmichael asked. "Are we going to take them back?"

"Of course," Mrs. Turner said. "The three of us can get the bodies up to the stage. Only twenty yards or so."

It took them twenty minutes to get the big driver's body inside the stage. They at last dragged him by the hands to the stage door. Then the three women boosted him through.

The salesman was easier. When they had the bodies in, they pushed them to one side, and the two women climbed in.

Emma Carmichael struggled up to the high stage-coach driver's seat. She gathered up the reins and tied them around the iron railing on the seat.

"Ready?" she called.

"Ready," the women inside said.

Mrs. Carmichael untied the reins, picked out the ones on the two lead horses, and slapped them on the animals' backs.

"Giddap! *Yaaaaaa!*" she called, and the two lead horses moved out. She pulled the leather lines on the lead mount's right side, and they angled back onto the dirt trail that served as a road.

She let the horses walk. Mrs. Carmichael felt much safer letting the six beasts walk, rather than run. If she did the wrong thing and they were even trotting, they might blunder off the road and tip over the coach, and then they really would be stranded.

They were less than ten miles from Red Bluff when the Indians attacked them. When the savages . . . She

8

felt the tears coming. Her baby was out there some-where. Her Kitty! With savages! How could it happen? That's why Fort Sanders was built a mile south of Red Bluff. How could the soldiers let this happen?

Tears came and she sobbed for a moment. Then she slapped the reins against their backs and walked forward.

Four miles an hour, she thought. Good thing she had been raised on a ranch and knew something about animals. Two hours, they should be near Red Bluff in two hours. Next time she would take the train, even if it was a lot farther that way.

Mrs. Carmichael shook her head. Get to the sheriff. Get to the Army. They would have a patrol out first thing come daylight, or she would scream at every officer on that post.

It was nearly three hours later when the coach rolled into Laramie. The time was after eleven P.M. The stage office had stayed open for them.

"Lord A'mighty!" the stage manager shouted when he saw a woman driving the rig. He ran up to the coach, and Mrs. Carmichael pulled the horses to a stop and tugged the long handle backward to set the front wheel brakes.

Larch Jones helped Mrs. Carmichael down. He recognized her.

"Mrs. Carmichael, what in the world happened? Where's Charlie, the driver? You're an hour late getting in."

"Indians," she said, then slumped toward him. Larch caught her and helped her to a chair in front of the stage station.

"Indians attacked you?" he asked.

"Yes, half a dozen or so. Killed Charlie and a man passenger, and then they stole away my Kitty, my four-year-old Kitty!"

9

"Oh my God!"

The other two women got out of the stage and stood by, nodding.

"Must have been ten or twelve of the savages," Martha Turner said. Shot down the driver, and then the drummer when they left. Took Kitty. You got to go tell the Army so they can go after them while the trail is still fresh."

"Can't do anything tonight, ma'am. Fort's all closed up. Getting toward midnight."

"I'm going. My husband will take me out there. I don't care what time it is."

"Charlie and the drummer . . ." Larch began.

"They're in the coach," Mrs. Carmichael said. "Get down my bags. I want to go home."

An hour later a buggy pulled up in front of the commander's office at Fort Sanders. A sentry on duty near the north side of camp had stopped the buggy and then led the rig to the front of the guardhouse, where Lieutenant Bevins, the officer of the guard, had listened to the civilians for a moment, nodded, and promptly led them to the fort commander's quarters.

Lieutenant Bevins knocked on the commander's door and waited. He knocked again and a third time before a light flared inside. A moment later the door opened and a face appeared.

"What the hell is going on?" Major Cliff Abbott demanded.

"Sorry to awaken you, sir, but Mr. Carmichael from town is here. There's been an Indian raid."

"The Cheyenne on the warpath? Don't seem likely. Hell, give me a minute to get my pants on and have him come in."

"Mrs. Carmichael is here, too, sir. The savages stole her little girl."

"Stole? . . . Bring them in, I'll get dressed."

Ten minutes later Mrs. Carmichael had told the major about the attack.

"You're sure they were Indians, Mrs. Carmichael?" the major asked.

"It was dark, they wore feathers, pants, I think. It was dark. They had bows over their backs. One man had a pistol, I know. Their horses had no saddles. I never saw any of them with long hair . . . but yes, I'd say they were Indians."

"How many were there?"

"I'm not sure, four or five, maybe eight or ten. They kept riding around and whooping and firing their pistols."

"You said one used some English; 'out' and 'lay on ground.' Did it sound like an Indian talking?"

"Yes, from what I know. It didn't sound like a white man. I've heard a lot of Indians now know some English."

"Yes, that's true. How far out was it from Laramie?"

"We walked the team for about three hours. About ten or so miles on the stage road south toward Tie Siding, where they got the ties for the railroad."

"I can't understand a sudden attack, Mrs. Carmichael. The Cheyenne have been quiet most of the summer. They haven't made a single raid I know of. They are hunting and making food for the winter and looking for buffalo. Also the spot you say they attacked you is over twenty miles from their camp on the Little Laramie River."

"Major Abbott. Are you questioning my wife's statements? She was there, man, she saw them. They stole our baby, and we demand that you do something about it. You can at least send out a patrol to be on the site by daylight so you can track the savages. My wife said they rode north on the stage road. Should give your Indian trackers a good start in trailing them."

11

"What you've told me doesn't seem like enough evidence. . . ."

"You have two dead civilians, you have a kidnapped child; what more do you want, Major, fifty dead civilians and half of Laramie burned to the ground?"

Major Abbott controlled his temper. He was a big, heavy man who had no trouble with his subordinates, but civilians were a strange breed to him. They didn't take orders well.

"I'm sure you don't mean that, Mr. Carmichael. We've kept the Indians well away from your mine, and at a considerable cost to this post. I'll talk with my best Indian scout and see what he thinks." Major Abbott pointed to the officer of the guard, who at once left the office.

"Major, may I remind you that I have a personal friendship with General Sheridan, and I will send him a wire the first thing in the morning, advising him of the situation here and encouraging him to press a campaign against the Cheyenne with all possible diligence."

"That won't be necessary, Mr. Carmichael," Major Abbott said. "I'll take care of it. I'll have a patrol ready to leave at 3 A.M., which will put us on site well before daylight. I'll have a report for you about the patrol's findings as soon as it returns tomorrow or the next day, depending on how far they can track the culprits."

He looked at the woman. "Mrs. Carmichael, I'm sorry about your daughter. We'll do everything we can to get her returned to you. Now, it's late, I suggest we all get some sleep."

Chapter Two

MARCUS QUINN AND his four companions sat at a table at the far side of the Elk Horn Saloon in Red Bluff, washing the trail dust out of their throats. They had been in town for two hours and made this the third stop right after taking care of their mounts at the Red Bluff Livery and then checking into the Transcontinental Hotel.

"We here on business, or just resting up a mite, Marcus?" Billy Joe Higgins asked. Billy Joe was a tall timber of a man, just over six feet five inches and lots over two hundred pounds. His long, wild red beard and unkempt hair often gave him a sinister look. But now his grin was a mile wide.

"Little of each. Still working out the details, but we got ourselves a goodly bit of business here, the way I figure."

Marcus was a tall man, slender, blond, blue eyed, and caught the eye of the ladies. His tanned face was clean-shaven and his hair neatly trimmed. He wore a trail-dusty pair of Confederate-gray trousers and a blue denim shirt.

He tipped his beer now, and for the third or fourth time Marcus glanced across the room at a table where one man sat drinking a beer and playing solitaire. The man had been staring at Marcus for the past ten minutes. His expression had grown angrier by the minute. Now he kicked the table aside and stood.

Billy Joe was huge, but this man was taller. He pushed aside the chair and lumbered forward.

Marcus looked away, but tensed.

"We got trouble headed our way," he said softly, yet loud enough so the other four could hear. Nobody looked up, but Marcus saw them all get ready, legs under them, hands off glasses, bodies tensed.

"You!" The voice came as an accusation, a challenge, an angry venting of stored-up fury.

Marcus ignored the voice.

"You! You little bastard in the blue shirt drinking with your four shifty friends. I'm talking to you, you murdering coward."

Marcus looked up slowly. Every man in the saloon quieted and watched the little drama.

"Somebody just fart in here, or is shit piled that high around here all the time?"

The huge man bellowed in outrage, drew his iron, and blasted a .44 slug into the floor near Marcus's foot.

"Stand up and draw . . . bastard!" the big man shouted.

"Penny, Penny," the barkeep shouted. "Take it easy. Don't go busting up my saloon again. You remember what it cost you last time."

Penny looked at the barkeep and shook his head. "I know this one. During the war. He come into our farm out in Kansas. Bastard shot two cows and butchered them. Then he killed my pa. He shot me, too, but I didn't die. Then he and his men ran off all our horses. I'm gonna kill him!"

"Sheriff won't take kindly to that, Penny," the bar man said.

14

All five of the men at the table stood. Billy Joe was closest to the mountain of a man with the six-gun.

Marcus laughed softly. "Penny, I never been in Kansas in my life. During the war I was out in California still looking for gold. Now you want to put away that little pistol and meander outside. I'll be more than pleased to see which one of us is best with a six-gun."

Penny squinted and turned his head, as if he heard better from one ear. The move caused him to look slightly away from where Billy Joe stood. The big man from Mississippi swung his left fist, backhanded, clubbed the .44 out of Penny's hand, and sent it skittering across the floor.

Billy Joe's long red beard shook as he jumped forward and pounded his big right fist into Penny's jaw, thudded his left into the towering man's belly, and then hammered another right fist into Penny's eye.

The three punches came so fast and hard that each backed up Penny a step. By the time he got his fists up, he was tottering. Billy Joe's fists crashed into Penny again, driving him back another step.

He stood there, shaking his head, then he swung. Billy Joe dodged the blow and kicked him in the shin, pounding his right leg out from under him and dumping him against a poker table, where some unfortunate jasper was just showing a full house with aces up.

Penny crashed right through the table and screamed in fury. He rolled over to his hands and knees and lunged upward with a hand clutching a chair leg.

In one of those quiet moments that happens every now and then in total bedlam, everyone in the saloon heard the deadly click as Marcus cocked his Colt .44 and leveled it at Penny.

"Piss-poor idea, Penny," Marcus said softly.

The big man looked up into the deadly black hole of the .44 muzzle and dropped the chair leg. He came fully erect slowly, one eye starting to swell shut, a bruise already showing on his jaw, and a look of murder on his face.

Billy Joe gathered up the gun Penny had dropped, opened the cylinder, and dumped out the five rounds that were there. He snapped the cylinder back in place and tossed the revolver to Penny.

"Like I say, Penny," Marcus went on evenly. "Anytime you want to put some rounds in that iron and meet me in the street, I'll be more than proud to oblige. Otherwise, you take a long walk on a short trail somewhere."

Penny grunted some half-whispered obscenity, turned with some difficulty, and glared at Marcus and Billy Joe before he pushed his handgun back in leather.

"I'll be back, you murdering somsbitches. I'll be back."

The barkeep watched Penny walk out the door and then went over to Marcus's table. He was a big man himself; nearly six feet and sturdy, with a lumberjack's shoulders and arms. He crossed his heavy arms over his chest above the white apron around his waist.

"You can count on him coming back, and when he does, I'm hoping you'll all be outside—back or front makes no difference to me—unless the five of you want to pay half the charges for broken tables, chairs, to say nothing of windows, mirrors, and heads that's gonna happen in here. Rather you did it outside."

Marcus stood and smiled at the bartender. "Then I'd say you're not putting us out, just warning us that when Penny comes back he'll have a few of his friends with him."

"I'd guess about ten from the mines. What he

usually does when he gets whipped. He does some enforcement work for Mr. Carmichael, who runs the Lost Man Gold Mine out a ways."

"It's a thanking you I'm doing," Marcus said. He nodded at the other four. "Friends of mine. I'd say ten to five is about the kind of odds we like."

The barkeep nodded. "A bit of the Irish here, I'd say."

"Two bits actually. We'll each have a new bottle of that beer and take it to the alley to accommodate Penny and his friends. We're new in town and we don't want to trash the streets with any broken-up mining riffraff."

"Damn, feels like old times," Hank Proudy said. He was nearly as tall as Marcus, the same age, and had dark hair that hung in soft waves below his ears. He was clean-shaven, except for a well-trimmed mustache. Dark brooding eyes stared at Marcus.

"Remember them eight guys we took on over in that little tavern in Copiah County? The time right near Christmas? We waded in broken noses and broken teeth that night."

"I remember; the Depro boys saved our skins at the last minute with some fancy knife and whip work."

The five had known each other since they were all about sixteen, growing up and getting in trouble back in Mississippi. One night they found themselves on the same side in a brawl, and that built them into a team.

Later they joined the Army when the war broke out, and quickly grew restless with the strict routine. A quick-thinking colonel put the five soldiers into a unique and self-contained unit and sent them north to raid behind the Yankee lines and provide all sorts of hell for the men in blue. They were called Quinn's Raiders.

The five Raiders took their fresh bottles of beer and moved out through the back door of the saloon to the alley. They at once looked for the strategic advantages and did not rule out the half dozen outhouses posted down the alley.

Near the end of the war a Texas colonel, trying to win favor with his Yankee captors, set up the Raiders to be captured. Soon labeled outlaws and killers rather than prisoners of war, they were sent by rail north to stand trial and to stretch five brand-new hemp ropes.

They escaped from the train, engineered by an explosion of three kegs of black powder, and were given up for "lost" and "dismembered by the force of the blast." They were officially dead.

Quinn's Raiders moved west, hunting new adventures and new grounds to plunder. They were responsible to nobody but themselves and to each other. Each man would die for any of the others. They formed a close bond that could be broken only by death.

Now they supported themselves by robbing trains, stagecoaches, and banks.

Now Quinn looked at the alley and at the men. He positioned them where he thought they could do the most damage. Bob Depro slipped out to his horse and brought back his bullwhip and settled in behind the outhouse twenty feet from the back door of the saloon.

Billy Joe had his Mare's Leg Springfield pistol-carbine hanging at his right side. The massive combination of a carbine and pistol could be shot as a pistol or with the stock on the shoulder. It held a .58-caliber bullet that could knock down a charging plow horse dead in the traces.

Quinn figured that Penny would be more interested in cracking skulls than shooting holes in them, so he would come with musclemen. Before Quinn could place the others, Penny came charging out the saloon back door with nine big men right behind him. None of them had guns out.

Penny stared into the darkness since his eyes hadn't adjusted yet.

"Where you at, you murdering bastard?" Penny yelled. A man behind him turned and pulled a six-inch knife. Bob Depro's bullwhip snaked forward and cracked as it wrapped around the man's wrist and jerked him off his feet, the blade skittering out of reach. Bob pulled back the whip and laced the man across the back, cutting his shirt open and drawing a line of blood.

Billy Joe charged at full steam, dodged past Penny, and slammed into the next four men behind him, dropping them like stalks of wheat under a scythe. Billy Joe rolled over and stood up in time to flatten another man with a wild haymaker that lifted the miner off his feet and dropped him unconscious three feet away next to the outhouse.

Marcus picked up an ax handle someone had thrown away and turned as Penny rushed toward him. Marcus sidestepped the giant's lunge and thrust the stick between Penny's ankles. He tripped over the ax handle and slammed into the dirt, roaring in rage.

Penny got to his feet and started to reach for his six-gun, then stopped.

"Killed my pa, bastard, I seen you!" Penny screamed as he charged.

"Never been in Kansas," Marcus shouted, avoiding a flailing right fist and thrusting the butt end of the ax handle into the big man's belly like a battering ram. It drove the wind out of the man, and he hit the dirt and rolled over a wet cow pie recently deposited by a team of oxen.

The fight had tallied down to one on one, with five of the miners already unconscious or dragging their way to the end of the alley, well out of the fight.

Loomis Depro had squared off with a man twice his size, but when Loomis drew his Bowie knife with its nine-and-a-half-inch blade, the big man moved back a step. Loomis drove in, feinted one way, then lunged the other way, and swung the big blade, ripping the man's shirt from side to side and cutting his chest.

The miner's eyes went wide, he bellowed in pain, and turned and ran for the street a half-block down the alley.

Bob Depro took care of two more of the miners; one who had just grabbed Hank Proudy in a bear hug. The bullwhip cut a six-inch slice across the miner's shoulder with the first swing. The second wrapped the end of the whip around the miner's ankle, and Loomis jerked the sturdy leather, dumping the miner on his back.

Two well-placed kicks in the ribs by Hank turned the aggressor into a broken and screaming man who wished he had never listened to Lester Penny.

Penny was having his own problems. He had backed up against a brick wall and was fending off thrusts from the ax handle. Then he saw what he wanted, a four-foot-long two-by-four, and took three hits to get to it. Then he charged Marcus, swinging the two-by-four with fury.

His first swing missed, and Marcus clubbed him in the thigh. It had no effect. The big man came on and swung again, this time slashing the ax handle out of Marcus's hands, stinging them like fire.

Now Penny grinned and glared through his one good eye. He stepped in and hauled back the two-by-four. The booming blast of Billy Joe's Mare's Leg convulsed the alley with a roar, and in the blink of an eye the two-by-four that Penny held slammed out of his hands and careened twenty rods down the alley, where it splintered into a dozen pieces when it jolted against a brick wall.

Penny's hands and arms felt as if they had been mangled. He hunched over a moment in anger and pain. Then, when he realized he could not fight with either hand, Lester Penny turned and called those of his crew who could still run, and they rushed down the alley.

"Casualty report," Quinn called.

"Nothin' ailin' that whiskey won't cure!" Hank said.

They all laughed and trooped back into the saloon. When they got to the door they found a crush of twenty spectators who fell away before them.

"By dang, they done it!" one of the onlookers called. "Done put them ten miners and old Penny running their asses off down the alley, and nobody even got shot!"

Inside, the several witnesses were recounting the melee when suddenly the whole saloon went quiet.

Marcus had just lifted a shot of the house special to his lips when he saw everyone looking at the man who had just come in the door. He was short and square, built like a five-foot-six-inch stack of bricks. His shoulders and arms were wide and strong, and he carried a hogleg with a ten-inch barrel that extended out the bottom of the holster.

The man cleared his throat, then looked at the barkeep.

"Evening, Bascomb. Hear you had some trouble in here tonight."

"Trouble, Sheriff Markowski? Nothing to mention."

"Heard Lester Penny went on the warpath, him and his ten pards from the mine."

"Oh, that. Yep, Sheriff. Lester was in here with

some friends. Seemed they all had to go out back together. I'd guess some of them are still in the alley, if you had a hankerin' to talk with them."

Markowski stared at the barkeep. "Better do that. Don't want nobody to leave here till I get back. You hear?"

He walked out the back door and the saloon returned to normal. Quinn's Raiders sat around the same table they had before. Loomis had found a deck of cards and had a game of solitaire started.

"He's gonna find one or two of them out there," Hank said softly to Marcus.

"Not our fault they fell down going to the outhouse," Marcus said, and they all grinned.

Bascomb hurried up to them. "You just saw our sheriff, Markowski. He's tough, but he's honest. He'll want to know what happened."

"Tell him," Marcus said. "Fair fight. Nobody got killed. Just settling a little argument."

The sheriff came back a few minutes later and stopped at the Raiders' table.

"Evening. You must be new gents in town. Here on business or moving on through?"

"Some business affairs to settle," Hank Proudy said quickly, affecting a slight British accent.

The sheriff looked up at hearing the accent.

"You're an Englisher."

"That's what you colonials insist on calling us. Is that against one of your laws?" Hank increased the accent this time.

"Not that you could get arrested for. What kind of business?"

"Confidential as of yet, I'm afraid. I hope that's not illegal, as well."

"No, sir. You have a name?"

"Quite. Sir Malcolm Davies at your service, officer."

22

"Must be cattle. All you Englishers think of are cattle." He looked at the other four. "The rest of you, any idea how those two gents out there hurt themselves?"

"I say, did they fall down going to the shitter?" Hank asked with his accent broader.

Everyone in the saloon roared, hooted, and laughed. When the noise died down the sheriff shook his head.

"Doubt it. One man has two broken ribs, another one is knocked silly, still unconscious."

"Quite serious, officer, I agree. You Yanks are so boisterous. I do remember something that happened yestreen."

Sheriff Markowski looked up sharply. "Here now, none of them foreign words. What's this 'yestreen' word mean?"

"Yestreen. Oh, jolly well sorry. Yes, bit of my Scottish heritage showing, I'm afraid. Word simply means last evening."

"Oh, what happened last night?" the sheriff asked.

"Well, let's see. No, officer. Upon further reflection, I'd have to say it has no bearing on this matter. In fact, it was involving a young lady of less than honorable virtue."

A few catcalls came from the listeners.

Sheriff Markowski frowned. "Englisher, don't you be making light with me. Could regret it and never see England again. Just want to set you boys straight. If you work for the Englisher here, fine with me. But anybody gets shot in this town, I get to it quick.

"We look on any discharging of a firearm in the city limits of Red Bluff to be uncalled for. City ordinance calls for ten days in the lockup, and you pay for your own food. Anybody gets wounded or killed, we apply the law downright stringent. Am I making myself clear, gentlemen?"

They all nodded.

"I say, good for you, Sheriff. Law and order and all that. Yes, I applaud you for that move. Could we set you up to a cold beer?"

"Thanks, but no. Don't believe in drinking when I'm on duty. But you can leave a tab at the bar with Bascomb for me." He turned and walked out of the saloon, and not a man in the place made a remark.

Marcus tipped his shot and emptied it. "I had enough fun for one night. I'm going to find out if that bed is as soft and inviting as it looked."

Hank drained his beer. "As for me, my bath water should be hot by now," he said, maintaining his accent. "If I'm lucky I'll find a small lass to scrub my back."

The rest of them nodded. They'd had a long day, and the soft beds did sound inviting.

Marcus caught the other four's attention with a glance. "I seen sheriffs like this one before. I'd suggest we go slow and cautious on any gunplay. We've got business outside of town coming up soon, and I don't want to have to bust any of you boys out of jail so you can come along."

∞∞∞∞∞∞∞∞∞∞∞∞∞∞∞∞∞∞∞∞∞∞∞∞ **Chapter Three**

THE NEXT MORNING at breakfast in a small cafe down from the hotel, Marcus heard about the kidnapping by the Cheyenne.

"Damn Indians snatched her right out of her mother's arms there on the stage road, I heard," a short man next to Marcus at the cafe's small counter said. "Gonna be a big announcement this morning by Carmichael."

When Marcus wasn't impressed, the older man went on. He had just finished a stack of hotcakes and bacon. He pushed the last half of a strip of bacon in his mouth and nodded.

"Hell, son, Carmichael runs the Lost Man Gold Mine up in the hills a ways. He's the richest damn guy in town. Only thing he can be announcing is a reward for the return of the little girl. Kitty, her name is."

"How much?" Marcus asked, quickly interested.

"Who knows? How much is an only child worth to an older man? I'd say in the thousands. Old man Carmichael is worth it."

Marcus worked on the rest of his food: three eggs, country-fried potatoes, half a dozen strips of bacon, three sausages, and two slices of toast. A ransom that

25

big was an idea worth considering. He had brought the boys to town with the set plan to relieve the mining company of the payroll due to go out to the mine from the railroad within a week or two. They had plenty of time before that.

"You gonna be in town long?" the old-timer asked Marcus.

Marcus turned to him and cut a piece of bacon in half. "Well, it just depends on how the wind blows and how the fancy ladies dance to my tune."

The old-timer stared slack jawed at Marcus for a minute, then grinned. "Gosh danged, I like that. Gonna remember that and use it one of these days." He finished his coffee, paid his tab, and walked out the door.

Hank and Billy Joe came in, saw Marcus, and the three of them took a table at the side. Marcus moved his plate and coffee cup over there.

"Morning, boys," Marcus said.

"Marcus," Hank said. He had shaved closely and used some of his cologne. He had on a town suit and white shirt and a vest he reserved for his hot gambling streaks. It was red and gold with real silver threads worked through it. It had cost him over two hundred dollars in Denver.

Hank glanced up and smiled as the waitress, a small girl with red hair and freckles and only the hint of breasts came over with a pad and pencil.

She looked tired already, even though it was only 6:45 A.M.

"Yes, gentlemen. What'll it be?" She said it automatically, then she looked at Hank and her smile brightened. She touched her hair, smoothing it back, and turned to Hank.

"Plateful like that one," Hank said, pointing to Marcus. "And coffee. You have any tomato juice?"

26

She didn't. She looked at Billy Joe and grinned. "And for you?"

"Quart of milk, three plates like he's got, eight slices of toast, and a pot of jelly."

She started writing, then looked up. "You joking with me?"

"No, ma'am, no joke."

She looked at Billy Joe again, lifted her brows, and nodded before she hurried back to the kitchen.

Hank and Marcus sat on one side of the small table, giving Billy Joe the other side as they always did. Marcus told them about the Cheyenne kidnapping and the possibility of a reward.

"Army sent a patrol out last night to be there at first light," Marcus said. "The word is, they'll try to track the hostiles. If it is the Cheyenne, that would be cause enough for them to mount a full-scale attack."

"If they can find the camp," Hank said.

"I'd heard that the Cheyenne in this area were settled down; hadn't raided a white ranch or killed any white eyes for over six months," Marcus said.

Hank sat stiffly in his chair, his eyes taking in everything in sight. "Well, you boys play nursemaid all you want." He patted his midsection where he carried a money belt under his clothes. "I still got some resources from our last little adventure, and I hear there's a fine gaming house just down the street. I may break down and try my luck with the cards later on."

Hank's food came then, and one plate for Billy Joe. The waitress looked at him.

"You want all three plates now or should I do it up hot for you?"

She watched Billy Joe forking down the food on the first plate. It was half-gone by the time she finished asking. She waved her hand and went back to the kitchen for two more plates and more jam.

When Hank left the table ten minutes later, Marcus touched his sleeve. "Remember, the law's tough here. Go easy with the hideout."

Hank bristled for a moment in mock anger. He was an actor again playing the Englishman.

"Really, old man. I am perfectly capable of taking care of myself."

The accent was perfect. He left two twenty-cent silver pieces and a dime for his breakfast and strode out the front door.

By noon that same day the cavalry patrol was back from the scene of the attack. The lieutenant on the patrol reported that there appeared to be only four horsemen, and that they did find an arrow and part of a feathered headdress at the site of the attack that were definitely Cheyenne.

The trackers had followed the attackers for a mile from the point where they shifted off the stage road into the open country, but they lost the tracks as they headed to the west.

Sheriff Markowski went to Fort Sanders to talk to Major Abbott after the patrol returned. Now he stood on the courthouse steps and made his report to thirty or forty townsfolk who had gathered there for the announcement by Mr. Carmichael.

"Major Abbott says his patrol reports that the raid may have been made by Cheyenne, but that there is not enough proof to send a force against the tribe camped on the Little Laramie. He feels that our town and the surrounding settlers are safe and that we should not worry about a Cheyenne attack."

There were a few questions, but the sheriff shrugged them off.

"You got any problem with what the Army says or does, you go talk to Major Abbott."

Marcus and Hank were both interested observers.

Hank had lost twenty dollars in a three-hour poker game and figured the money well spent.

Hank looked at Marcus. "What do you make out of the Army report?"

"Sounds true enough to me. Be interested to hear what the Depro brothers think."

A few minutes later, H. Wilson Carmichael came from the courthouse to the steps. The crowd had increased to over a 150, with every bar rat and out-of-work logger, miner, and cowboy on hand to hear about what was hoped would be a chance to earn a fortune.

Carmichael was about average height, dressed well in a dark blue suit and vest over a white shirt. He wore a formal blue tie and sported a gold watch chain and fob across his vest. He had a full mustache and muttonchop sideburns that extended to his jaw line. Carmichael looked to be about forty-five, slightly overweight.

When he marched out on the steps, he was visibly angry.

"Fellow citizens of the fine town of Red Bluff. I have just been told by Major Abbott, who is supposed to be protecting us from the savages, that they are not certain that the Cheyenne stole my baby and killed two men last night on the road south."

He glared at everyone. "What the hell do they know? My wife was there. My wife was shot at. My wife saw two men die last night at the hands of the savages. My wife had our four-year-old daughter ripped out of her arms by one of the painted, feathered, bareback-riding Cheyenne warriors!"

He stared at them.

"I know you people. We're neighbors and friends. I've lived in this town for over eight years. I know it was the Cheyenne. As of right now, I'm offering a reward of twenty-five thousand dollars. . . ."

There was a swelling of talk from the throng below him.

"A reward of twenty-five thousand dollars for the safe return of my daughter Kitty. I'm not looking to punish anyone for this crime against humanity. But if the savages find themselves on the wrong end of a .52-caliber rifle round or a .45 slug, I won't cry any tears over it.

"That's all I have to say. The reward will be paid in gold as soon as Kitty is returned to her mother and me. May the good Lord help you in finding Kitty, and help her to stay safe."

He walked back into the courthouse.

When the crowd scattered, Billy Joe and Bob Depro and Loomis Depro joined the other Raiders. They leaned against the hardware store.

Bob Depro and Loomis were brothers; one-quarter Choctaw Indian from Mississippi. Their mother had been a half-breed and had to raise the boys herself. Both were dark, showing their Indian blood, and Loomis had a crescent-shaped scar on his left cheek. Loomis got it in a knife fight with a Cajun and his dirk. The Cajun marked Loomis for life, but before the fight was over the Cajun's life was through.

Both men wore their hair long, Indian style tied at the back in a ponytail. Bob wore buckskin trousers and a feather in the band of his wide-brimmed, low-crowned black hat. Loomis stuck to puncher trail gear, except for a necklace of Indian beads given him by his mother. Once he killed a man who taunted him about the beads.

Bob was older and more muscular than his brother. He had a feeling for animals, and could deal with them on a level no white man could. Both young men were acutely aware of their Indian heritage.

Marcus nodded at the Depro brothers. "You heard

what the sheriff said, and that yankee Major Abbott. You boys reckon it was the Cheyenne who stole the child?"

Bob laughed softly, shaking his head. "Not if these Cheyenne are like the other plains Indians we dealt with. The Cheyenne got two great loves; fighting and horses. No Cheyenne warrior worth his shield would raid a six-horse stagecoach and leave behind the horses."

Loomis nodded. "Yep, six horses to any Cheyenne warrior are worth twenty times what the small girl child is. They would steal the horses first, then look at the captives. The driver was shot out of the seat and the other man killed later. There was no battle."

"They wouldn't have left the three women, neither," Bob added. "If they looked strong and could work, they would have taken them as slaves or maybe wives. Otherwise, they probably would have raped and then killed them. That's the way the Cheyenne warriors live."

"Besides," Loomis said, "the three women would be worth much more than one small girl child."

Marcus nodded. "Wouldn't the Indian scouts with the Pony Soldiers have told the Army this?"

"Even Arapaho or Pawnee scouts would have told the lieutenant on the patrol this," Loomis said. "It don't make sense that Indian scouts couldn't track four horses. No one even said if the mounts that raided the coach were shod or unshod Indian ponies."

Hank snorted. "Looks like the Yankee bluebellies are simply washing their hands of the matter. They could at least tell the civil authorities what they found."

"It ain't certain they learned nothing," Marcus said. He rubbed his jaw a moment in thought. "I think we should wait a day or two. If Carmichael gets a ransom note, then we'll know it isn't the Cheyenne. If he doesn't get a ransom demand, it still could be the Cheyenne."

Just then the sheriff of Albany County came out on the courthouse steps. He bellowed out a greeting and waited for a few people to gather.

"Men, as sheriff of Albany County, I'm authorizing a posse to go out and follow the trail of the kidnappers. I can take up to twenty men. We'll be leaving in an hour from the alley behind the courthouse. Bring a rifle and fifty rounds, a pistol and fifty rounds, and water and food for five days. Blankets, of course. Furnish your own mount and the county will pay you a dollar a day. Two hours from now, right behind the courthouse."

Half a dozen men yelped in delight and ran for their horses and home for some food and gear.

Billy Joe looked up at Quinn. "So, are we going with the posse?"

Marcus shook his head. "We wait and rest up. I figure that posse won't find much."

Loomis scowled. "One thing they will do is mess up any trail that might have been laid by the killers. It means we'll never be able to track them after twenty horses charge over the real trail."

Marcus held up his hands. "Right now we wait."

Sheriff Markowski did not like riding a horse. Still he led his fifteen volunteers on the trail. Three hours later they had found the tracks in the middle of the little-used stage road and followed them back to where the hostiles turned off the stage road and headed west.

"Heading into Indian country," Willy Belcher said. Willy was the sheriff's top deputy and the best tracker in town. Willy followed the trail for three hours, and the sheriff figured they had covered about ten miles.

"Halfway to them heathen," Willy crowed. A half hour later he lost the tracks. He scratched his head.

"Them damn tracks went straight ahead into this little creek, but they never come out on the other side," Willy said.

"Went up- or downstream to lose us," Sheriff Markowski said. "Send two men along the banks each way, and you'll find them tracks."

A half hour later, the two men moving upstream fired one pistol shot, and everyone charged their direction.

Willy looked at the tracks coming out of the water. They were in the soft ground along the bank.

"Damn, this is a single set of prints and the prints ain't shod. This a damn Cheyenne war pony for sure!"

The sheriff frowned. "You mean the prints we've been following are made by horses with shoes on them?"

"Why, sure, Sheriff. Lots of injuns have shod horses. Capture them from the cavalry. Now they ain't about to rip the shoes off a horse. Ruin its hooves that way." He looked back down at the tracks.

"But this one here's different."

He had just said it when a rifle snarled and Willy pitched backward, a large red stain showing on his chest, where a high-powered bullet had slammed all the way through him.

"Take cover!" the sheriff bawled. He dove behind a cottonwood and waited. There were no more shots. He counted his troops. He still had fourteen left.

"Anybody see where that shot came from?" the sheriff bellowed.

"I saw smoke up there, two hundred yards to the left," someone said.

"Put a couple of rounds in there and stay under cover."

Every man in the posse fired, and the blue smoke around the men was thick enough to choke on.

"Cease fire!" the sheriff bellowed.

They saw an Indian headdress lift up a moment, then pull down quickly behind a log near where they had been firing.

"Bastards!" the sheriff growled. "I saw them. Indians by good goddamn. Two more rounds up there, everybody!"

Sixty rounds thundered into the spot where the Indians had been seen. After the barrage, a single shot answered them. It tore through a man's leg that had slipped into the open from behind the cover of a cottonwood tree trunk.

"I'm hit! Christ, tore half my leg off!" the man screamed.

Sheriff Markowski saw the problem. He had a bunch of civilians here and he'd stumbled into a war. He pointed at six men who had the best cover and a retreat path.

"You six, get that wounded man and shag your tails out of here. Move it now. Stay low so they can't find you." The sheriff called to the other men. "I want a shot up there at them savages every fifteen seconds or so. Keep them busy. We're pulling out of here. Damn savages got the high ground and we got nothing here."

Shots began sniping up the slope at the spot where the Indians were seen. No more shots came from above.

A half hour later the sheriff laid covering fire as the last man crawled and then ran down the slope into a heavier stand of aspens and some Engelmann spruce that gave good cover.

The sheriff darted ten feet ahead into the open, grabbed Willy Belcher's foot, and dragged him back to cover.

"Made it, by damn," the sheriff said. Then he

hoisted Belcher's body on his shoulder and worked back down to his men.

"We're going home," he told the posse. "Came up here to find out if it was the damn Indians, and we proved that. Now it's up to the Army to fight the war."

They rode cross-country toward Red Bluff and came back to town just after dark. Sheriff Markowski took Belcher's body to his house and gave the man's wife and family the sad news. He helped lay out the body on the dining-room table and then knocked on neighbors' doors so they would know and could comfort the family.

Later that evening the sheriff rode down to Fort Sanders and told Major Abbott what he had seen and the reception he had gotten when he started following the tracks into the Indian-controlled territory.

The major took notes as the lawman talked, and said he would report the incident to the Army Department of the Platte headquarters in Omaha by telegraph. He made no assurances that his troops would move in and attack the Cheyenne, though.

Word of the posse's fight with the Cheyenne spread around town within minutes after the men rode in. Marcus heard it as he had a beer in the Elk Horn Saloon. By then the story had grown to three killed, including two Cheyenne.

Bob Depro had vanished upstairs two hours before with a big-breasted blonde who let him get his hand on the merchandise before he paid.

Hank looked over at Marcus when he heard about the posse coming back. He had just won a pot with forty dollars in it and now was no time to quit the game. Three other men pushed their cards to Hank to deal. He chose five-card draw and passed out the cards.

Loomis left the table to talk with a man who had

been on the posse. He was spending his dollar on nickel beer. Loomis talked to him for ten minutes, then came back.

"Was it Indians they tangled with out there, Loomis?" Marcus asked.

Loomis shook his head. "Don't know. That feller was in the posse. Said they followed the tracks almost to the timber, then lost them in a stream. Some other tracks were unshod and probably Cheyenne, but he don't know if they were the same ones."

"Did he see any Cheyenne out there?"

"He said he saw some headdress feathers. That was all. He said they shot only twice from the heavy cover. Both shots hit their marks."

Marcus laughed. "Doesn't sound like Indians to me. Loomis, you ever seen a plains Indian who was much of a marksman?"

"No. They shoot many times, hoping. The man said the ones shooting were not on horses, they were dismounted among some rocks and trees. He said it looked like a fort, almost. Like they was waiting for somebody to show up."

"Cheyenne don't fight on foot if they got their horses," Marcus said. "This is starting to smell bad."

"Trouble," Loomis said softly, nodding his head toward the door.

Marcus looked up and saw Lester Penny walk into the saloon. He still had a bruise on his cheek. The swelling had gone down from his eye so he could see out of it, but the surrounding flesh was deeply purple. He looked at Marcus for a moment, then turned away to the bar.

He got a beer and walked toward the table where Marcus sat. Loomis stood halfway in front of Marcus, pulled out his Bowie knife, and began cleaning his fingernails with the tip of the nine-and-a-half-inch blade.

Penny stared at Marcus for a long moment, then at the big knife, and he turned and sat down at a table with his back to Marcus.

A half hour later, Marcus got up and he and Loomis walked over to the poker game where Hank had just cleaned out the last man. He pocketed the money, gave the barkeep five dollars for the use of the table, and they left, heading for the hotel.

"What do you make of the posse's little war?" Hank asked.

"Cheyenne don't fight that way," Loomis said.

"Someone trying to blame the Cheyenne for the kidnapping?" Hank asked him.

"Looks like. The stage holdup was not the way Cheyenne warriors work. The horses were even shod, the posse member told me. The headdress the sheriff saw is easy to fake or steal. Cheyenne don't lay in wait for a posse to follow a plain-laid trail."

"Boys," Marcus said, taking out a cheroot and lighting it, "I think we got us some planning to do."

Chapter Four

IN THE FRINGES of the foothills leading to the Medicine Bow Mountains, where the first mighty ponderosa pines grew, where a sprinkling of Douglas fir began to take root, and where there were a few Engelmann spruce, Slade's four white men flaunted the Cheyenne feathered headdresses, so they were sure that the big sheriff's posse below would see them.

They had laid the trail carefully, honed the deception, and led the posse directly where they wanted them. Then all they had to do was wait. It happened the first day.

Flinch had the honors of blasting the first man. He took out the tracker with one round from his Henry repeater and sent him jolting toward heaven or hell.

The four crouched down behind the stone work they had piled up along with some old pine logs when the flurry of return fire came. Not a round got through.

Slade had drilled the second posse member when he let his leg slip out from behind the protection of the cottonwood. He grinned as they watched the posse move off down the small valley and out across the gentle hills that ended in the grasslands.

"Can I fire off a few more rounds at them?" Flinch asked. "Know I could scare hell out of them from here."

"Dammit, no, Flinch. We done what we needed to. We killed one and wounded one, and that stupid sheriff is gonna say it's the Cheyenne, for sure. We're playing for high stakes here. We're going for thousands in ransom, and that's not even counting a river full of gold dust."

When the posse was out of sight, the four men stood and faded back into the better timber, where they had left their horses. They rode three miles to the hidden cabin.

They had nailed the cabin door shut from the outside when they left that morning. Now Possum pulled out the nails, and they went inside.

Kitty sat on a bunk playing with some charcoal on a pad of paper she had found. She was black from the charcoal but not hurt. Possum started a small fire and got some food ready.

"We got one problem," Slade said. "Information. We don't know what old man Carmichael is doing or saying." He looked at the three men. "Which one of you had been in town the shortest time?"

Dirk at last raised his hand. "Me, I reckon."

"How'd you like to go into town and get a cold beer and listen to the talk?"

"Damn right!"

"Leave right soon. Find out what the sheriff is saying. Find out what the Army is doing. They should be ready to raid them Cheyenne by now. And see if there's any kind of a reward offered for the little button over there. We want to hold off at least a week, or maybe two, so the price will go up, and so the damn Army will wipe out the fucking Cheyenne on the Little Laramie."

39

Dirk put a blanket roll together and collected some food he could take along.

"You ain't going on a hundred-mile trip," Slade barked. "It's only a little over ten, twelve miles in to Red Bluff from here. Travel light. I'll even give you some spending money. No playing poker. Have a few beers and listen good. If you hear of anybody else heading this way, get your ass on your horse and pound back out here so we can set up another little surprise."

"Right, boss. I got it. What about that beer money?"

Slade gave Dirk a five-dollar gold piece.

"Now don't lose it, and bring back all you don't spend. You might need to stay the night. No whores, and no whiskey. Just a few beers. I don't want you stinkin' drunk."

"I got it. Hell, I won't leave the barn door open, not when there's that big reward involved."

Dirk rode out. It would be dark before he got to town, but there should be plenty to listen to.

Slade got some water and a cloth and washed the small girl. He had to keep her halfway presentable for the big ransom. He wished they'd taken her carpetbag as well, but Indians don't rob stagecoaches of the luggage.

The little girl had become a good camper with them. She had stopped crying and seemed to take her captivity in stride. She smiled and sang a little song and played with some pinecones they brought her. She even insisted on Slade helping her say her prayers when he put her to bed that night.

After that they waited.

Dirk came back the following day at about two in the afternoon. He had been riding hard, and his horse was lathered and almost used up.

He staggered up to the cabin and collapsed on the porch.

"More coming!" he gasped. "Get me some water. I ran out."

"Who's coming?"

"Three of them. Two mountain men and an out-of-work miner. They got good rifles and plenty of rounds. The miner was along yesterday with the posse, so he knows the spot. They're coming for the reward."

"What reward?" Slade asked.

"Carmichael put up a twenty-five-thousand-dollar reward for the safe return of Kitty."

"That will bring a dozen wild men charging up here, heading for Cheyenne country," Slade said. "They'll all be spending that twenty-five thousand dollars before they earn it." He walked around the cabin. "They will, unless we can stop them cold."

"How?" Flinch asked.

"We play Indian again."

An hour later, Slade and his men took the three riders by surprise. They caught them a half-mile below the previous attacking point so that they wouldn't be ready for trouble.

Slade told his men not to kill any of the three. First they had to capture them all alive. Wound them, but not kill them.

The four hid on one side of a draw as the trio worked their way up. They had seen them coming five miles away and planned the attack carefully.

Slade took the first man, Flinch the second in line, and Dirk the third. They were to wound them only. Shoot them in the right shoulder so they couldn't shoot back.

The others would fire after Slade had. The bushwhackers were ahead of the trio of riders, and when they came to thirty yards away, Slade fired at the big

man in the high-crowned brown hat. The round jolted into his right shoulder and spun the man off the
horse.

Almost at once two more shots blasted into the high
country's silence. Both of the riders were hit. One fell
off his horse, the other one draped over the mount's
neck and hung on.

Dirk had dressed up with all of the Indian costum-
ing they had: a feathered headdress, moccasins, a
loincloth. They had painted his face with colors to
disguise it, and rubbed clay into his skin to make him
look darker.

Now the bushwhackers waited to see which
wounded man passed out first. The shot-up men
screamed and bellowed in pain, but none of them
could move. The moment they tried, another bullet
slammed into the dirt near them.

The smaller of the three fainted after five minutes.
All had seen Dirk running from tree to tree, threaten-
ing them with a lance. When the first man passed out,
Flinch yelled.

"Now? Is now the time?"

Slade told him it was and Flinch calmly shot the
two men who were still conscious. He killed them
with head rounds.

The four armed men moved up cautiously. Slade
checked the unconscious man and quickly tied his
bandanna around his eyes in a blindfold. Then they
tied his feet and ankles and put him back on his horse
and led him up into the trees.

Slade had prepared a spot. A big cottonwood had a
limb that would hold the bodies of two men. They
stripped the dead men of their clothes, threw ropes
over the limbs, and tied the ropes to the corpses' feet.
The bodies were hauled up until their heads hung
eighteen inches off the ground. Then the ropes were
tied off.

Slade whistled as he built small fires directly below the heads of the two corpses hanging head down.

Flinch brought up the man who was still alive. He had come back to consciousness, but was still blindfolded. No one spoke during this time. Slade built up the fires until the flames burned the hair off the corpses' heads and blackened their skulls.

Slade nodded when they were ready. Three of the men faded into the woods, hid, and watched. Dirk, in his Indian costume, led the blindfolded man forward and untied the survivor's ankles, then his hands.

Dirk grunted and made strange sounds as he did this. When the man's hands were free, Dirk stepped back. At once the man pulled the kerchief off his eyes. The first thing he saw were his two friends six feet in front of him, roasting over Indian torture fires. He screamed. He turned and threw up. Then he saw Dirk and crawled away.

"White eye," Dirk said with a guttural accent. "Go!" he said, pointing. The man saw his horse and rushed toward the mount, looking behind him, his right arm dangling useless at his side.

He fell twice, then made it to the horse and lifted on board. His right shoulder was shot up and still bleeding, but it wouldn't be fatal. The man looked at Dirk once more, then pulled the horse's head around and bolted downhill and away from the terror of the two white men roasting over torture fires.

Nobody moved near the bodies until the rider was a mile away. Then all four broke out laughing.

"Did you see the expression on his face when he saw his two buddies hanging head down?" Slade roared. He left the bodies where they hung as mute evidence for any other reward hunters to find.

They got their horses and rode back to the cabin, about five miles away this time. They had set up their torture scene closer to the Cheyennes' camp.

"Damn, this should get the Army into action," Slade said. "That poor sombitch is gonna yell his head off to the Army, to the sheriff, and to everybody else he can get to listen."

"Next time somebody else gets to be the Indian," Dirk said. "I'll never get this dirt washed off me."

On the way back to the cabin, Slade decided they needed an ear in town again. "I'll go into town this time," Slade said. "We need to know just what's going on in Red Bluff. It ain't time to give Carmichael a ransom note yet, though. We got to get the Army moving against them damn Cheyenne!"

It was close to dark when Nathan Laibrook rode into town with blood dripping off his elbow. He went straight to the doctor's office and banged on the door.

Young Dr. Teague hurried to the door, saw the blood, and led Nathan into his treatment room, which was part of his home as well.

"Shot?"

"Yeah, doc. Could you have somebody go get the sheriff? I got something mighty grisly to tell, and I want him to hear it, too."

Dr. Teague sent one of his small sons to fetch the lawman, then cut Nathan's shirt away and checked the wound.

"Least the bullet came out. Could have killed you. Guess it just wasn't your time. You won't be riding around the countryside for a while."

The doctor put some ointments on the wound, splashed on some alcohol, and winced when Nathan screamed louder than he did when he was shot.

"If it hurts, it's healing clean and proper," Doc Teague said. He bound up the wound and put a wrap of bandage around Nathan's shoulder and upper chest and then offered him the ruined shirt.

Sheriff Markowski came in, saw the bandaged shoulder, and sat down heavily in a nearby chair.

"Your name is Nate something," the lawman said.

"Nathan Laibrook, Sheriff. Me and two friends went up toward the Little Laramie River area, looking for that little girl. You won't believe what happened."

He related the story from start to finish and said he had seen at least one savage, and it was the same one who helped him get away.

"You sure they were Indians?"

"Sheriff, I've lived in this county twenty years. I know what the Cheyenne look like, painted or unpainted. This one even knew some English. Don't ask me why they didn't build three fires, though."

"Your two friends dead?"

"Glory yes, Sheriff! The fires had burned off their hair already and charred the skin on their heads. They were also black with soot. Fire leaping almost up to their necks. Only thing I didn't see was their skulls exploding."

The sheriff stood up. "Come on down to the office. I want to write this all out, so you can sign it. Then we'll go down to the fort and you can tell Major Abbott."

"Yeah, I guess I got to. First, though, Sheriff. First we got to stop at a saloon for two good stiff shots of whiskey."

Everyone in town knew about the latest Cheyenne atrocity before the survivor finished talking to Major Abbott.

The major listened, as did his chief scout, a Dakota who spoke English passably.

"Mr. Laibrook, are you *certain* that the person you saw was an Indian?"

"Major, he was reddish skinned, he wore moccasins, he had feathers on his headdress, he had a loincloth. He sure as hell looked like an Indian."

45

The major turned to the Dakota and spoke softly for a moment, then turned back to the civilians.

"If they were Indians, and tortured and killed your two friends, why would they let you go? That's not like a Cheyenne warrior on the prowl."

"I don't know," Laibrook said. "I just know I'm shot but alive, and they're hanging head down over those fires."

"I'm sorry about your friends, but there's nothing we can do to help them. My advice to you and all other civilians is to stay out of that section of the Medicine Bows until we get this straightened out."

"Can't you send a patrol in there and look around?" Sheriff Markowski asked.

"If I think we need to, we will. Right now, none of my scouts have reported any hostile action at all by the Cheyenne. That's Hawk's Eye's band up there, and we never had any trouble with them. He controls his people well."

"Major, how do you explain the kidnapping from the stage, the Indians who attacked my posse, and now this double murder, all with definite signs and witnesses who saw Indians, including me?"

Major Abbott stood and walked to his window. "Sheriff, let's say a robber stormed into the Red Bluff Bank. His gang stole only the two- and three-cent pieces out of the cashboxes, and ignored the twenty-dollar gold pieces and, say, ten thousand dollars in U.S. greenbacks. Wouldn't you think that strange?"

"Damned peculiar, yes."

"That's what the raiders did at the stagecoach. My scouts laughed when I told them. They said no Cheyenne warrior would ever raid a stagecoach and leave behind the six horses. Horses are the measure of wealth, power, and prestige for the plains Indians.

"My scouts say as well that raiding Cheyenne would

46

have stolen the women first to use as slaves, then the child last, not left to drive the stage on into town."

"I'll be damned. Why didn't somebody tell me this before?" Sheriff Markowski said.

"You probably didn't ask, Sheriff. It's a thousand-to-one shot that the stage was hit by Indians. More likely whites dressed up to look like Indians. Their main purpose looks to be kidnapping the little girl."

"Then why blame it on the Cheyenne?" the lawman asked.

"That's what we've been trying to figure out. Your confrontation with the riflemen, and this attack on three civilians looking for the small girl could all have been staged to appear to be Indians."

"M'god!"

"Major, I was there. I saw those men hung over Indian torture fires. How could a white man ever do such a thing?"

"Mr. Laibrook. Remember, it was the white man who taught the Indians to take scalps for pay."

"We don't need a damn history lesson, Major," the sheriff growled. "Looks like my best deputy got killed for nothing."

"Not necessarily, Sheriff. When we find these outlaws, we'll hang them for sure."

Back in town, Marcus heard about the latest "Indian" victims as he had an early-evening haircut. The barber stayed open late because he had nothing else to do. He was a talker. By the time he finished trimming Quinn's blond locks, Marcus knew the whole story.

He met Hank and Loomis in the Elk Horn Saloon and talked it over.

"Possible," Hank opined. "But why the hell let one man go?"

The other Raiders looked at Loomis. He shrugged. "Not like a Cheyenne warrior. If two is good, three fires would be better. But more important, why would the white man who escaped see only one Indian? The whole band would be there."

"Another attack made to look like Indian work," Hank said. "Why in hell is somebody dumping shit on the Cheyenne?"

"Usual reasons," Marcus said. "They want the land where the Cheyenne are camped."

"If they wait for two months, the grass will be used up in that spot and the band will have to move," Loomis said.

"Two months is a long time if you're greedy," Marcus said.

"At least the Army hasn't charged up there and slaughtered the Cheyenne," Hank said.

Loomis scowled and shook his head. "Not yet."

Bob lifted his brows. "Might be worth a ride into the Cheyenne camp to find out what they know about the situation."

"If we could get in without getting a dozen arrows through us," Hank said.

Loomis grinned. "What do you mean 'we,' white man?"

They all laughed and Marcus began to nod. "That's a good idea. If the Cheyenne don't have the girl, somebody up in the hills does. All we have to do is find them and bring the little lady home."

"For twenty-five thousand dollars," Hank said.

"So first we talk to the Cheyenne," Loomis said. "They probably don't have scouts out since they aren't at war. We might be able to walk right into their camp."

"And three of us wind up head down over a bright, blazing cookfire," Hank said.

"No chance," Loomis protested. "I heard around town this band is led by a peace-minded chief called Hawk's Eye. I'd say we should go pay him a friendly visit."

H. WILSON CARMICHAEL PACED up and down on the wide porch of his town home, looking out over the best part of Red Bluff. Damn it! He'd half built this town, put hundreds to work in his mine, and now he couldn't get the sheriff to do a thing for him.

The damn major out at the fort was worse. At least he had some influence with important people back east. He'd call on them if that was the only way.

He had heard about the third incident; the two poor men roasted until they died over a fire. Barbaric! If he had his way, every Indian in the west would be shot down and dropped into a huge common grave. Get rid of all of the animals at once!

But the bleeding hearts around wouldn't hear of it. They were even converting some of the heathens to the church. What an insult! He almost stopped going to the congregational when that happened.

Carmichael jammed his derby on his head and called for his rig. It was time he went to see the major again. Three incidents were too many to ignore. If there wasn't an immediate patrol sent into the area, he would telegraph General Sheridan.

A short time later, H. Wilson Carmichael sat in the

commander's office. Major Abbott stood behind his desk. Beside him stood a much shorter man, an Indian by the looks of his leathery face, his long black hair, and his dark eyes. He wore the shirt of a cavalry corporal and tan pants. His gaze evaluated the civilian.

"Mr. Carmichael, I'd like you to meet Running Dog, my chief scout. He knows Indians as well as any man in the West. Tell him about the three incidents, Running Dog, and what you think about them."

Running Dog's English was not perfect, but in six or eight well-chosen sentences he explained to the mine owner that the raids were not conducted by Indians, that the Cheyenne were not on the warpath, and that all three incidents were undoubtedly the work of white men disguised as Indians.

"Whatever for? Why would they do that?" Carmichael railed.

"Mr. Carmichael, you're a mine owner. Would you have any idea why someone might want the Cheyenne out of the Little Laramie River system?"

"Well, since you put it that way, yes, there could be someone wanting in there for the land, to check for minerals. But not me, I'm too busy right where I'm at. I'm not behind any of this, if indeed some white men are.

"Regardless of that, I am demanding that this fort send a patrol in force into the Cheyenne camp area to check on the hostiles." He glared at the major, putting the full force of his personality behind his demand.

"We have no reason to think they have committed any hostile act," Major Abbott said. "Your request is denied."

Carmichael's face grew red around his mutton-chops. His eyes closed down to slits and he set his jaw. He was not used to being countermanded.

"Very well. This afternoon I'll be sending several telegrams. One will go to John M. Schofield, the secretary of war, urging him to have the area checked for hostile activity. And I'll cite the three violations by the Cheyenne. I'm also going to wire the Speaker of the House, Schuyler Colfax, and the president of the Senate, John J. Ingalls.

"My fourth telegram will go to the military division of the Missouri headquarters in Chicago and General Phil Sheridan. We were schoolmates once, and he has great faith in my opinions.

"In short, Major, you'll be hearing from men who will insist that you make the patrol that I have requested."

Carmichael turned abruptly, charged out of the office and to the parade ground, where he waved for his driver to come. He stepped into the fancy carriage and raced away with a pair of matched and prancing black mares pulling his rig.

As he rode back to town, he noted that this was another day passing with no ransom demands. That alone was proof enough that the Indians had captured his Kitty. There would be no ransom note, and they would corrupt her and disfigure her, cut off her long hair, and try to raise her as a Cheyenne Indian. The very thought made him want to vomit.

That afternoon all five of the Raiders grouped around a table at the Elk Horn. The Depro brothers were getting restless. They disliked staying in one spot more than a few days unless there was some good reason for it.

"When we gonna *do* something?" Bob Depro asked. "What we waiting here for?"

Billy Joe chuckled. "Must mean you ain't found the right big-titted blond whore yet, Bob. You just keep looking, she's here somewhere."

Hank had been shuffling a deck of cards he had

found on the table. He neatly cut the cards with one hand and sprayed them out on the table in a fancy fan. Then he looked at Marcus. "What's the drill, Marcus?"

"I say we go see if the Depros can walk us right into the Cheyenne warrior camp. We want two days to see if the ransom note comes in, and if it don't we head out to find the girl."

"Sounds good to me," Marcus said. "Gives me time to make a few dollars on the green felt of a crap table."

"I'll go down to the livery and check out our horses," Loomis said. "About time they had a good feed of oats."

The other two drifted off as Marcus worked on his beer. Bascomb came up just after the last man left. He looked at Marcus.

"Penny says he's gonna kill you. Figured you should know. It can't happen in my place. Sheriff closed down the last saloon where there was a killing. Had it shut up for a month. Damn near busted the place."

"Penny a back shooter?"

"I'd figure so."

"If he comes in, you tell him—" Marcus stopped and stared at the entrance. Lester Penny walked in. He wore two guns and came directly for Marcus's table. "Never mind, I'll tell him myself."

Quinn stood up, pushed his outside jacket behind his six-gun, and lifted the leather hold-down loop off the hammer. Then he scowled.

"I hear you're a back shooter, Penny. That true?"

"Only on rattlesnakes like you, Quinn."

"Not here, Penny. I'd wind up in jail for killing you. You got a horse?"

"Two of them, right outside. Just you and me."

"And you've already got your three riflemen in position to make it a really fair fight, right, you tall pile of shit?"

Penny lunged at him, but Marcus stepped back out of his way.

"Outside, both of you," Bascomb ordered.

Marcus downed his beer, pointed to the door, and Penny walked ahead of him. Outside, Marcus looked around quickly. He saw no obvious ambushers.

"West along the tracks," Penny said. He pointed to the two horses. They both mounted at the same time.

"Not west, we'll go down to the river south of town. Fewer uninvited guests that way."

Penny began to sweat.

"You don't like the river?"

"Anywhere is fine, Quinn. You'll die just as quick down by the water."

They rode in silence. No one followed them. Marcus kept a good lookout but could see no one who might be ready to turn and shoot him in the back. Soon they galloped a quarter of a mile and eased up as they came to the river a half-mile south of town.

"How you want it, quick or slow?" Penny asked.

"I want a Texas walk-down."

"Never heard of it."

"Big gunfighter like you should know all about the Texas walk-down. Each man has one round in his piece. We start forty yards apart and walk toward each other. Either man can fire whenever he wants to."

"But just one shot each?" Penny asked.

"Right. Soon as a man fires, he stops walking. If the first shooter misses, the other man can walk down as close as he wants to before he fires. Walk right up and put the muzzle over the other guy's heart and blast away."

"Sounds damn strange. First one who fires better hit his man, right?"

"True, or he's the dead one," Marcus said.

"Suits me fine. I never miss."

"Fine, first we'll check each other's weapons," Marcus said. He drew his six-gun slowly, opened the cylinder, and pushed out four of the five rounds and pocketed them. He held up the weapon so Penny could see the empty chambers.

Penny did the same thing to his weapon, then both men carefully holstered their six-guns.

They walked away from each other, both checking over their shoulders to see that the other wasn't about to do some back-shooting.

When they turned and faced each other, Marcus gave him one more chance. "We don't have to do this. I don't have a blood feud with you. You just ease up and don't go around threatening me, and we can both walk away from here."

"Not a chance. I said I'm gonna kill you."

"Remember, the man who fires first stops in place," Marcus said.

As he stared at the gunman facing him, the familiar calmness came over him. For a moment he was at peace, relaxed, rested. He knew that his whole life hung by the slender cord of his next act. He either lived or died by the accuracy of his revolver and his aim. It could all be over in a fraction of a second after the other's weapon fired.

They both began to walk forward. Each took deliberate steps. Each held his right hand close to the butt of his revolver. They began at about a hundred feet apart. By the time they were at fifty feet, Marcus drew his revolver and lifted it.

"Go ahead, shoot," Penny shrilled. "Too damn far and you know it."

They walked closer. Most gunmen liked to get within twenty feet of their opponent before firing. Revolvers never were very accurate.

They were at forty-five feet. Marcus felt sweat pop out on his forehead.

They were forty feet apart. Penny drew his weapon and carried it at his side.

Two more steps. They were at thirty-two feet.

Now!

Marcus stopped, set his feet wide apart, refined his sighting, steadied his hand. He braced his strong right hand with his left and he saw Penny's surprised look. The other man's six-gun started to rise, so he could sight in.

Marcus's fingers squeezed slowly, tightening evenly, no jerk, no pull. The weapon went off. Through a small cloud of blue smoke from the powder, he could almost see the flight of the slug. He saw it hit Penny in the chest and stagger him back a step.

The big man did not fall down. His face showed pain for a moment, then he grinned. He didn't speak, just started walking forward, step by step. He was unhurried.

Marcus frowned; his aim had been true. He had hit the big man in the chest. Had he missed the heart? It would be the last mistake of his life.

Penny had lowered the weapon as he came closer. Now he was at twenty feet, now eighteen. He came forward, his face a bright smile, his eyes wild with the power, the thrill of victory.

Fifteen feet.

Penny lifted the weapon now, steadied it, and held it chest high as he came forward again.

Ten feet.

Penny grinned. "Thought you had me," he said softly. "Thought you'd killed me!"

Eight feet away.

Penny took two more steps and laughed softly. His eyes were black holes now, angry, staring. His breath came in quick gasps from the tension.

He lifted the weapon and aimed at Marcus's heart.

Six feet.

Four feet.

The muzzle of the weapon rested on Marcus's chest, over his heart.

"Good-bye, Quinn," Penny said. Then a thin line of blood showed at his mouth. His finger strained to pull the trigger. His eyes closed, then struggled to open. They did, and he tried to push the weapon forward.

A second later his eyes closed and he toppled sideways, the final gush of air coming in a death rattle from his lungs.

Marcus swallowed hard, shook his head to clear it. He had sung his own death song as the Comanche would say. He had escaped death by a fraction of a second. If Penny had chosen to fire when he was eight feet away, instead of squandering another three seconds moving up and then talking . . .

Quinn holstered his weapon, then thought better, drew it and filled five of the chambers with rounds, then eased the hammer down on the empty one. He walked over to his horse slowly, mounted, and rode across a shallow place in the stream and north toward town. He went past the main section of the village and came in from the north. Tying the horse where he had found it, he walked across the street to Elk Horn.

He motioned to Bascomb. The apron who also owned the place set him up a nickel beer.

"I've been here all afternoon, best you can recall, right, Bascomb?"

"Near as I can recall, Mr. Quinn. If you pay for that beer." His eyes sparkled with unasked questions. "I'd say we won't be having to worry about—"

"Won't be having to worry about any rain for the rest of the week, you're right, Bascomb." Marcus took the beer and went over to a nickel-limit poker game

57

and sat in. Poker is not a game where you can lose your money quickly, like roulette or dice. It's a fine game to fill up an afternoon, where four or five men will swear that you've been playing.

AFTER AN EARLY supper with the Raiders, Marcus
prowled the stores that were still open. He was in the
Red Bluff Hardware looking for a folding pocket
knife, a small one that wouldn't take up much room in
his pocket. As he checked over the knives in a display
case, two women came up arguing.

They stopped just across the aisle from him, and he
couldn't help but hear them.

"I don't care what you say, Agnes, it just stands to
reason. The poor woman hasn't had a ransom note. It
has to be the Indians. Why would some white men
steal that darling little girl and not send a ransom
note?"

The woman talking was small and insistent, her
voice loud and clear. The second woman was taller
and slender, and her arms were now crossed over her
bosom.

"That just can't be true," Agnes said. "We try to
blame everything on the poor Indians. I have never
seen an Indian harm another human being. Now
come on, admit it, Blanche, you haven't, either."

"I haven't seen the Pacific Ocean, either, but that's
no reason to say it ain't there. Agnes, you're just plain

stubborn about Indians. Just 'cause your uncle was a missionary with some heathen out in Arizona for a time."

"Got nothing to do with that at all, Blanche Greggory."

Marcus took off his hat, turned around, and stepped toward the two women.

"Ladies, would you mind if I jumped into the argument? I've had some contact with Indians. I hate to see two such pretty ladies carrying on so right here out in public. Both of you seem to be dead set in your opinions. Maybe I could help a little."

Agnes looked at him a moment, then glanced away. Blanche took more time. She grinned.

"Well, howdy, you're the one who had that little fisticuffs with Lester Penny, aren't you? Your guys whupped their guys was the way I heard it. Oh, scuse my manners and all. I'm Mrs. Blanche Greggory, and this is my stubborn schoolteacher friend, Miss Agnes Ballard. She's the one who was standing up for the Indians."

"I'm Marcus Quinn, and I'm right honored to make the acquaintance of both you fine ladies. Indians. Seems strange subject for you to be quarreling about."

"We weren't quarreling," Agnes said, looking up at him from soft blue eyes. "We were just having a . . . a discussion."

"Well now, one thing I like is to discuss. Perhaps I could provide a cup of coffee for you ladies at the cafe next door, and I could enter into this discussion."

"Oh, I'm afraid . . ." Agnes began.

Blanche rushed in with her acceptance. "Why, that does sound right friendly. Agnes and I would just love to have some coffee. This shopping is so exhausting."

"Oh, I really don't think that I can," Agnes said.

"I've been around a lot of Indians. Know two like brothers, and I've even fought against a few."

"You fought against Indians?" Blanche asked. "Oh, how exciting. You must tell us just all about it. Agnes will be happy to come, because if she doesn't, then I can't, me being a respectable married woman and all."

Blanche shot an angry glance at Agnes and poked her in the arm until she relented.

"All right, but just for a few minutes. I do have classwork to get ready for tomorrow. . . ."

"I understand," Marcus said. "I even went to school once myself."

He escorted them next door, forgetting the pocket knife. They sat at a small table, where Marcus put his back to the wall from long habit.

"I believe you were talking about the Cheyenne and the chances that they kidnapped the Carmichael girl," Marcus said when they were seated.

"It's absolutely impossible to believe," Agnes said. "Why would Indians come all that way for a child? It doesn't make any sense."

Blanche looked at Marcus.

"Well, it would make sense to the Cheyenne. Most Indian women have one or two children. They look at white settlers with eight or nine children with envy. Many tribes in the plains, especially, do steal children —white, Mexican, and from other tribes—to bring into their tepees and raise as their own children."

"Mr. Quinn, you're making this up," Agnes said.

"No, I'm afraid not."

"So, Miss Schoolteacher, you just might be wrong," Blanche said. "The Cheyenne stole Kitty, after all."

Marcus grinned and shook his head at Blanche. She was dark and tiny and feisty, and her breasts were large for her small body.

"Mrs. Greggory, I didn't say that. The Cheyenne would understand stealing children. They didn't steal Kitty, I'm sure of it."

Agnes took a long breath and stared angrily at Marcus. "I know they didn't. Why do you think so, Mr. Quinn, Indian expert?" Her cheeks turned pink with her anger. Her small mouth tensed and her chin came up a little.

Quinn sipped his coffee. "When the coach was attacked, the warriors would have taken all three women along with the child to use as slaves or wives."

Blanche sat back smiling. Agnes sat up straight, her coffee and small cookie forgotten.

"But someone stole that poor little girl. There hasn't been a ransom note. If the Cheyenne didn't steal her, who did?"

"I'm sure the sheriff would like to know the answer to that question. I don't have the answer. All I said was that I knew something about Indians."

"That's what you said," Agnes shot back. "Did you know the Indians have been living here before the white man? Did you know that the U.S. Army is slaughtering the Indians at such a rate that in another twenty years there might not be a single Indian left?"

"That might take some doing, Miss Ballard," Marcus said.

Blanche stood up suddenly. "Oh, my goodness. I have to rush right down to the Stitch-Sew Shop before it closes. I'm out of pink thread. You two just go on with the discussion, I'll be back directly and keep up my part."

"I should go as well," Agnes said.

Blanche put her hand on her shoulder, holding her in the chair. "Why, Agnes, you said you had practically nothing to do tonight. Now you just relax, and let me get my thread, and I'll come right back. I just love to have these discussions."

She hurried away.

"If you do have to go . . . ." Marcus said.

"Well . . . no, I guess not. You . . . you said you have some Indian friends?"

"Yes, brothers. We ride together. They're only one-quarter Choctaw."

"Choctaw, that's a tribe deep down in Mississippi somewhere, isn't it?"

"Yes, you get a grade A on that answer. Nine out of ten western people never heard of the Choctaw."

"I have studied the Indians and their problems. We are literally stealing their birthright, their nation right out from under them. I hope you realize that. The federal government has no right to give land away to the railroad, or to sell it or let people homestead it. That's all Indian land. They have been on it for hundreds and hundreds of years."

They went on talking, and at last the owner of the cafe came up and told them she was closing. It was almost eight o'clock.

"Oh, my goodness, it's dark out and everything," Agnes said. "Blanche never did come back."

"Miss Ballard, I'll be glad to escort you home. It's quite dark out there."

She watched him a moment. Evidently making up her mind that would be the simplest, she nodded and stood. He held the door open for her and they walked along the boardwalk on the commercial street.

"Oh, I'm up here two blocks," Agnes said, pointing north at the second corner. After the first half-block, there were wood frame houses on both sides of the street. The house they stopped at was small, painted white, and had a white picket fence around it.

"The house . . . it's part of the salary for the teacher. It isn't big, but it . . . it serves my needs quite well."

She opened the gate and he went past it with her up to the porch. There were two steps.

63

"You have a key?"

Agnes smiled. "No need, anyway the lock is broken. Here in Red Bluff almost nobody locks the door." She hesitated. "Would . . . would you like to see my book on the American Indian?"

"Yes, I would."

She opened the door and led him inside.

"You stay right there and I'll find the lamp."

Marcus took matches from his pocket and lit one, flooding the room with the faint light.

She brought a lamp from the dining-room table and he used another match and lit the wick. She put on the glass chimney and turned up the wick.

"There, now we can see where we're going." Agnes sighed. "Oh dear, I really shouldn't have asked you in."

"It will be our little secret, Miss Ballard. What about that book?"

She took it from a shelf and spread it on the table. It was large and well printed, but at once Marcus could tell it was more than half-myth and what some easterner thought the Indians were all about.

"Most of this isn't true," he said bluntly.

She looked up, surprised. "What on earth do you mean?"

"This part where it says the Plains Indians will soon learn how to raise crops and domesticated livestock. The Cheyenne are a warrior tribe. The men will never stoop to digging in the ground or stringing fence."

"You're making that up to win your argument, Mr. Quinn."

"No. It's the truth. Warriors are fighting men. They will help butcher and dry buffalo meat after a big kill, but that's only because if they don't, much of the meat will spoil. If they don't get it dried in three days, it's no good."

"Would . . ." Agnes looked away. Then she turned

back, her face soft in the lamplight. "Would the Cheyenne really have killed the three women on the stage if they had attacked it?"

"Absolutely. Killed them or captured them as slaves or wives."

"Good Lord." She turned, and her small fists came out and she hit his shoulders. He tried to stop her, and at last caught her hands.

"No, I won't believe you. You're making this all up."

He held her hands.

There were tears in her eyes. "Please let me go." He let go of her hands and put his arms around her. She didn't try to move.

He bent and kissed her lips. She didn't respond. He held her again and pressed his lips to hers, and this time she moaned softly and kissed him back.

She sighed. "You know I shouldn't be doing this. I could get fired. . . ." He kissed her words silent and held her close. He moved her backward to the sofa and sat down with her. As they did she fell into his lap.

She looked up at him, waiting to be kissed again. He pressed his lips to hers, and as he did his hand moved over her small, hard breast.

"Oh, no," she said softly, not meaning it. Then his lips captured hers again. He fondled her breast gently, then with more pressure, and she broke off the kiss and smiled at him.

"Now I could really have my contract canceled." She leaned up and kissed him quickly, licking his lips with her tongue. "And you know what? I don't care."

Marcus worked his hand slowly past two opened buttons on her dress and felt under some other cloth, then his hand closed around her bare breast.

"Oh, that feels so delicious!" Marcus moved then, lifted her carefully, and headed toward a closed door.

"The other door," she said, her eyes half-closed. He

toed it open and saw the bed in the faint light. The shades were down. He lay her on the bed, kissed her lips, then her breasts through the fabric.

"I'll get the lamp," he said.

She hadn't moved when he came back. He lay on the single bed beside her. She was on her back and he kissed her and found her breasts again. Then he unbuttoned the dress. She nodded and sat up and took it off over her head, along with her chemise and wrapper.

Her breasts were small and firm with rosebud nipples on small areolas of pink. He bent and kissed them. She responded. He kissed them again.

"Hmm," she whimpered and tore into a long series of spasms that shook her like an aspen leaf and made her reach for him and pull him over on top of her. When she finished, sweat beaded her forehead. She sat up, staring at him in surprise.

Quickly she tore off the rest of her clothes until she was naked, then yanked at his boots, and helped him undress. When they lay side by side, both naked, she rolled over on top of him.

"How can you be so handsome and so dangerous all at once? One hint of this to the school board and I'm on the next train."

She took saliva in her hand and coated his erection, then she positioned herself just right, guiding her throbbing slot down and swallowing up his staff to the hilt.

Nestling her breasts against his chest, she began a slow rocking motion that set Marcus on fire. He rolled and bounced with her, and a moment later she was riding him like a cowboy on an unbroken horse.

She climaxed but barely slowed down as she worked at him to bring him to his orgasm. She used her inner muscles now, squeezing him with fingers that vaulted him forward, and sent him crashing into a brick wall, shattering his body and his mind. His hips thrust upward a half-dozen times, then six more until he was drained and spent, and she fell on top of him.

Neither of them moved for ten minutes. They both panted and gasped for air and tried to regain their strength.

Agnes lifted up a few inches to focus on his face. "Damn, I feel as if I've died and gone to heaven."

He tightened his arms across her back. She bent and kissed his lips, then she buried her head in his shoulder and nibbled his flesh.

It was four A.M. before Marcus pulled his pants on. Agnes had fallen asleep, exhausted from their night of loving.

He kissed her, then slipped out, went down the alley, and ten minutes later found his hotel. The night clerk was sleeping as he walked quietly up the steps and into his room. It was locked the way he'd left it.

Marcus crashed onto the mattress and went to sleep at once. He didn't wake up until nearly noon.

∞∞∞∞∞∞∞∞∞∞∞∞∞∞∞∞∞∞∞∞∞∞∞ **Chapter Seven**

JUST BEFORE SUNRISE, three men slipped up on a small ranch eight miles due west of Red Bluff on Burnt Creek. Slade and Possum watched the chimney spout smoke.

"Breakfast time," Flinch said. "Wonder what they're having for their last meal?"

"We do this quick or slow?" Possum asked.

Slade laughed. "Depends on how good lookin' the woman is."

"What difference, she's a woman," Flinch said.

"Not a fuck of a lot of difference," Slade said, and all three of them laughed quietly.

The screen door swung open and a man came out. He stretched, then headed for the small corral at the side of the barn.

"Mine," Flinch said. He looked at Slade, who nodded. Flinch brought up his Remington and sighted in. A moment later the rifle cracked, and the big slug ripped through the young rancher's chest, dumping him backward into the dust.

The door opened again. A woman screamed and ran into the yard, dropped down by her husband, and looked around. Tears streamed down her face.

68

"Bastards!" she screamed. "Cowardly bastards! Come out and fight like men, not damn cowards from ambush. You killed a good man!" She jumped up and ran back into the house.

Slade grinned. "Go burn down the barn and the outhouse," he ordered the other two. "This little woman is mine."

He jumped up from behind the stack of firewood where they had lain, and ran for the house, zigging back and forth.

Two pistol shots sounded from the back door. Neither round came close. He made it to the side of the wall when the woman came out with the big Colt in her hand. She aimed it directly at him, holding it with both hands, and pulled the trigger. Slade dove to one side.

The hammer fell on an empty chamber.

She screamed and threw the revolver at him and started back into the house. Slade surged up from his knees, ran forward, caught her around the waist, and picked her up and continued on into the small house.

She clawed at his face.

Slade slapped her and she quieted. She was young and slender with good breasts. He caught her blouse and jerked downward. The fabric tore, showing her large breasts, half-covered by big pink areolas and strawberry-tipped nipples.

She spit in his face. Slade slapped her again.

"Now, little woman, you just be good and I might be nice to you. You had a real man's good hard cock lately?"

She glared at him. Tears came again. "Buck was a good man, and you killed him for nothing! We got nothing here to steal! He'd a told you that. Damn you!"

"Things happen," he said. Slade shoved her forward to the side of the one-room cabin where an iron

bedstead sat. Slade pushed her down on it and parted
her legs. He was hard and ready.

Slade ran his hands up her legs, and he saw her try
to fight it. She swung her fist at him, and then her hips
bucked forward. He pushed her skirt up to her waist,
ripped open his pants, and dropped down between her
legs. She seemed too submissive. He found the soft
brown hair over her treasure. She jolted when his
hand brushed her crotch.

"Oh, yeah!" Slade said, looking at it. He dropped
down and drove at her, digging deep, finding the slot,
and ramming in hard and fast.

"Oh, damn!" His dry skin pushing past hers hurt
for a moment, but then her lubricant flowed and he
laughed as he plunged in and out of her.

He was building up faster than he wanted to. He
needed to make it last longer. He held himself up with
one hand and grabbed her big tits and squeezed them,
rubbed them hard. He felt her move under him and
checked her, but she was just squirming.

"Like that, do you, missy? Damn good cock I got.
Yeah, you like it good!" His pressure built. He closed
his eyes and pumped hard. She moved again and he
figured she was liking it more. Women were all the
same once you get a cock in them, he decided.

Then she screamed. The sound came just as a knife
plunged into his side. The pain felt the same as the
time he had been bayoneted during the war. His hand
whipped up to the wound and found the blade.

He pulled out of her and went to his knees, looking
at his side.

Blood spilled down from the stabbing. "My own
knife! You bitch!" He slapped her, but as he did his
side hurt. He looked again. The blade was two inches
into his side, just below his ribs.

Gingerly, he touched the hunting knife. He grabbed
her torn blouse and wadded it up, then pulled the

blade out and pushed the cloth against the wound as fast as he could.

Moving the knife brought a gush of screaming from him that he couldn't stop.

"Slade, you all right?" Flinch asked from the cabin door.

"Dammit, no. Bitch knifed me. Come in here and make her pay for it."

Flinch chuckled. "Barn's on fire. We run the five horses out of the corral and let loose some chickens and two old cows. Yeah, this little pussy looks like she needs milking—right now."

Flinch had his pants open and fell on her, grabbing both of her hands and pushing them over her head. He chewed on her breasts until she cried out.

"Hurt my pard, will you? I know what to do for you." He entered her roughly and never stopped until he grunted twice and came out of her.

"Yeah, I done her once," Flinch said.

Slade had watched with interest. Flinch had climaxed so quickly. "Yeah, now find a sheet or something and tear it up to make a bandage. Wrap me up. Then call in Possum. He's got to get some of this poontang."

Five minutes later, Possum came in the cabin and grinned when he saw the naked woman. Slade had cut her skirt off and thrown it off the bed.

"Get on your hands and knees, bitch!" Slade ordered. The woman's eyes were glassy, frightened. "You'll do anything right now to stay alive, right, woman?"

Slowly she nodded.

Possum stood there drooling. Slade laughed. "Get your prick out of your pants and take her from behind, Possum. And don't say I never gave you anything."

Possum dropped his pants and mounted the woman. She promptly fell on her chest on the bed. Possum didn't seem to mind. He rode her down to the soft bed and kept pumping. He found the right spot and pumped away, his hands working under her until they caught her breasts.

"Oh, God," Possum bellowed. He laughed and gave one final pump with his hips and came away from her.

"Damn, but you're as fast as a fourteen-year-old," Slade said. He turned to Flinch. "Search the place for any cash. A cookie jar, maybe an old tobacco tin. Something under the mattress."

He sat the woman up and watched her breasts jiggle. "Damn good tits. We should take you with us . . . but then you'd just cause problems." He turned to Possum. "Go plant them damn arrows and feathers and that broken lance. We been here too long."

After ten minutes of searching, Flinch showed Slade a tobacco tin with some silver and two gold coins and some greenbacks.

"Good work. Help Possum. I'll be out in a minute."

Flinch left after grabbing the woman's breasts for one more feel, then he went out.

Slade fondled her breasts, brought his hand up her leg, and pushed a finger up her slot. He didn't want to leave her. He pushed her down and finished what he had started, blasting his seed deep into her, jolting her up on the mattress with every hard stroke.

He climaxed and roared in victory, then he grabbed her breasts. "You really want to stay alive, don't you, little bitch?" She nodded at him, her eyes wide, her pretty face showing her fear.

"No such luck. You like a knife so much, you can have it."

He plunged the six-inch blade deep into her stomach. Her eyes went wide, and she cried out softly, her eyes unbelieving. For a moment she held out a hand to him, then her eyes glazed over and she shook her head slowly.

"Hurts, don't it?" Slade asked. Then he leaned back and jerked the blade out. He lifted the bloody knife and in one quick stroke, slashed her throat from side to side. She toppled backward on the bed, her right carotid artery spurting heartbeats of blood all the way to the ceiling as her heart labored to fill her tubes with the life fluid. She was dead by the time Slade walked to the front door. He trashed the kitchen part, then hurried outside.

Flinch had just jammed one Cheyenne arrow with a hunting tip into the bullet hole in the man's chest. It looked good. Slade took a second arrow and slanted it between her ribs and rammed it four inches into the cooling body.

He saw the barn burned halfway down already and the outhouse burning. They were ready to leave the house.

The three hurried back to their horses, which had been kept out of the yard. They mounted and rode away to the west, then split up to make three trails.

"See you boys tomorrow," Slade called. "I'm going to stir things up in town. Take care of that kid. She's still our big payday, even before we find the gold."

He turned and rode for town. He had wiped all the blood off the knife, and would wash it when he came to the Laramie River just outside of town. It was a two-hour ride.

When he got to town, he stopped at the sheriff's office and pushed open the door.

Sheriff Markowski looked up. "Yeah?"

"Sheriff?"

"Right."

"Just rode in from the west. When I was well by it I

saw a good-sized smoke out about eight, ten miles.
Didn't go back and look. Didn't think I could do
anything to help. But I figured you should know. Been
any Indian raids around here lately?"

"Not to speak of. Who are you?"

"Lonnie Marshall. Just getting into town. Is there a
good hotel here?"

"Only one; take your choice. Why did you mention
Indians?"

"I come through the edge of the Medicine Bows and
thought I saw a few warriors far off. I turned and
pounded the trail for three or four miles. Never saw
them again, which is probably why I still got my hair.
That was about sunrise."

The sheriff nodded. "Just wondered, Marshall. I'll
send a couple of men out there to check. Two or three
small ranches out that way. Thanks."

"Welcome, Sheriff. Now I'm hankering for some
good grub." He turned and walked out of the office
and led his horse down the street to the hotel. He
might even have a bath. He remembered the feel of
the ranch woman's soft breasts, the way she moved
when he had entered her.

Slade shook his head and went inside and registered
and ordered a bathtub and four buckets of hot water
brought to his room.

It was nearly five o'clock that same afternoon before
the pair of sheriff's deputies got back from the smoke
report. They talked to the sheriff for ten minutes, then
all rode south for a mile to Fort Sanders.

Major Abbott listened to the report of the two
deputies.

"Yes, sir, Major," Deputy Wilson said. "The white
male in the yard had two arrows in him. We brought
them back. Figure they're Cheyenne. Didn't see no

bullet holes. The barn was burned to the ground and the woman was raped, then stabbed, and had her throat slashed.

"She was inside the cabin on the bed. Don't guess they had any kids yet. Young couple, maybe twenty."

"You're sure all the horses were gone, and any milk cows they had were gone?"

"Yes, sir. We seen lots of tracks near the corral, and the gate was dragged open."

"Any sign of shod horses?"

"No, sir. No new prints in the yard. We did find boot tracks, but the rancher wore boots, too. . . ."

Major Abbott scowled. "Now, Sheriff Markowski, this one does sound like a Cheyenne raid. They came for horses, they got horses, they violated the woman, and they killed her. That's Cheyenne.

"We'll have a company-sized patrol heading out at first light to check the place and to try and pick up any tracks. If we don't find any, we'll figure the Cheyenne took the horses one by one on twenty different trails. They get real crafty that way. We'll proceed into the Medicine Bows within five miles of the Little Laramie, but we won't make any contact with the hostiles if we do need to get any closer. I'm not about to start up the Indian wars again. Best we can do for you."

Just before five-thirty that same afternoon, Loomis and Billy Joe checked their horses in the livery. As they came out, they were yelled at by three off-duty soldiers.

"Hey there, breed, what the hell you doing in white-man country?" one soldier called.

A cavalry corporal laughed. "Why, he's just checking on his ancestors. Most Indians are half-horse anyhow, way I hear it."

Loomis turned and stared at the soldiers. All three

were bigger and heavier than he was. Billy Joe pushed
past Loomis and walked up within spitting distance of
the blue-shirted troopers.

"You boys trying to get your heads busted?" Billy
Joe asked.

The tallest of the three put a pocket knife away and
stood up tall.

"Hear tell you think you're a big man," the tall
soldier said. "Look soft in the gut to me."

Billy Joe grinned, putting on his simpleton act. He
looked back at Loomis. "Depro, he talking bad about
me?"

One of the troopers laughed. Billy Joe stepped
forward and slammed his big fist into the soldier's
jaw, jolting him backward over a pile of hay. Without
waiting a split second, Billy Joe threw his left fist into
the second Army man's belly, doubling him over. The
third man jumped back out of range.

He looked over at his two buddies. "Come on, guys.
Just one of him. The breed ain't fighting. All at once."

The first trooper got to his feet unsteadily, the
second one coughed out the last of his bellyful of fist,
and all three charged.

Billy Joe took a crack on the jaw and a solid right to
the stomach. He hardly noticed either blow. With one
massive arm he swept away one attacker, hitting him
in the side and nearly breaking him in half. He lay in
the dirt of the street, retching from the kidney blow.

The second soldier drove in headfirst. Billy Joe
raised his knee and caught the man on the side of the
head, slamming his head upward and to the rear,
straining his neck, and putting him out of action.

The third soldier reached for his pistol, firmly
planted in the leather holster on his right hip.

Loomis Depro's thin knife drew blood across the
back of the soldier's hand just as it closed around the

six-gun's handle. The trooper screamed and let go of the gun. Veins on the back of his hand gushed blood as the man grabbed his right with his left and bellowed in pain.

"Bastard!" the soldier screeched. "We'll be back. You two won't get away with this. We'll be back with our whole damn company!"

"I hope some of them can fight better than you three," Billy Joe said. "Hell, we didn't even get up a sweat. You little-boy campers get out of here and send back some men."

The three limped down the alley. Billy Joe made sure they didn't pull their revolvers. When they went around the corner a block down, he and Loomis walked on toward Main Street.

"He shouldn't have called you names," Billy Joe said.

"And you should let me defend myself. I could have handled all three of them."

Billy Joe grinned. "Sure, I know. I just wanted to have some fun." He frowned. "Also, I didn't want you to stick one of them bad and get us in trouble."

Billy Joe was the enforcer of Quinn's Raiders. He grew up in Mississippi with the rest of the group, and soon his strength became well known. Once he lifted a wagon to free a wheelwright who had been working on it when the blocks holding it up slipped.

On a drinking bout over in Hinds County he had taken on the sheriff and three of his deputies, and single-handedly put them all down and out of the fight. Some people said Billy Joe killed a plantation overseer up in Issaquena County in Mississippi for raping one of his young cousins.

When the three soldiers limped back to the fort that evening, the sergeant of the guard was called. After having the one man's hand bandaged up, he found out what happened. The sergeant made a report to the officer of the guard, who reported it to the adjutant.

"Sir, we've got to do something about these damn civilians ganging up on our troopers," Adjutant Stallone told the fort commander. "Tonight three of our men were beaten up and slashed by a gang of ten civilians. We just can't put up with this kind of disrespect."

Major Abbott frowned. "Captain, don't believe everything that an enlisted man tells you about a fight in town. When I've followed up on these reports, I've found that half the time the fault lies with our troops. If you want to stop it all, simply restrict the men to the fort."

Major Abbott checked a paper on his desk. "You have that patrol assigned and provisioned for tomorrow morning?"

"Yes, sir. B troop will be heading out with Lieutenant Vuylsteke."

"Good. That's all, Captain."

≈≈≈≈≈≈≈≈≈≈≈≈≈≈≈≈≈≈≈≈≈≈≈ **Chapter Eight**

QUINN'S RAIDERS ATE around the same big table in the Plains Cafe, where they usually wound up for food.

"Billy Joe here will have a side of beef, medium rare," Hank said as the girl took their order. Billy Joe grinned at the good-natured ribbing.

"Not likely," Billy Joe said. "But I would like about three orders of that beef stew and six slices of bread and a quart of milk."

The waitress knew not to question Billy Joe anymore. When she had the last order she left, and they all looked at Marcus.

"Hear about the raid on a ranch only ten miles out of town?" Marcus asked them. The Depros hadn't. He filled them in about it.

"Now, this time it could have been Cheyenne, with the horses all run off and both the whites dead and the barn burned down," Bob said. "Sounds reasonable."

"Tomorrow morning we're going to head into the hills and find out for sure," Marcus said. "I'm getting tired of lying around town. We'll leave sometime after breakfast. No rush. We'll take food for five days; pick it up tonight or in the morning. Then we ride for the Cheyenne."

"Anybody have any idea where Hawk's Eye's camp is on the Little Laramie River?" Marcus asked. He looked around, but no one helped. "So we'll hit the river fairly low and follow it up. They'll be up high on it somewhere."

"My guess is that they'll find us first," Loomis said. "It's important not to fire at them. If we want to show that we're friends, we need to demonstrate it."

"Warning shots over their heads might be a good idea, though," Marcus said. "At least we can get their attention that way before they kill us."

"Depends whether we find a couple of hunters first or a war party coming back from a raid somewhere," Loomis said. "Let's hope it's a single hunter."

Hank toyed with his steak, which was not characteristic of him. Marcus noted it and asked him if anything was wrong.

"I'm just not sure we can trust this Carmichael. Think I'll get a top hat and go call on the sheriff and then Mr. Carmichael himself, just to confirm that twenty-five-thousand–dollar figure. Can't hurt anything."

"Can't hurt a thing," Marcus said.

A half hour after the supper, Hank stepped into the sheriff's office. He wore a dark blue suit, a conservative vest, a watch fob and gold chain, but no watch, which didn't matter because a watch wouldn't show, anyway. His top hat was right out of an English society picture.

Once in the office he removed the hat and held it in front of him as the sheriff looked up.

"Oh, yes, our own Englishman, Malcolm Davies, as I recall."

"An excellent memory for names, Sheriff. Could I have a confidential word with you?" Hank asked, keeping his accent moderate.

"Nobody else in here."

80

Hank sat down in the chair beside the sheriff's cigar-and-bullet-scarred desk.

"It's about that reward for the safe return of the Carmichael girl. Can we take the man's word on the amount? I have known men to renege on an offer such as this."

The sheriff stood and walked around a minute, puffing on a short, fat cigar. "Why?"

"You see," he said, clearing his throat, "I have raised a group to go into the foothills to the west. Of course, we want to be assured of payment. We'll do our best to find the small one and bring her back, but first I'm going to pay a call on the distraught father of the child."

"He's good for it, if that's your meaning. But it might be a good idea to talk to Carmichael yourself," the sheriff said. "Get it out in the open; what you'll do, what he'll pay."

Hank stood. "Thank you, Sheriff. It's been good talking with you and to receive your suggestions. Next time we meet, let's hope we have good news for Mr. Carmichael."

Hank nodded at the lawman, turned, and left, a slight grin on his handsome face as he went out. Maybe he should give up all this fun and go to New York to become a stage actor. He certainly enjoyed fooling these locals.

Twenty minutes later he stepped from the fanciest coach for rent in Red Bluff and stood in front of H. Wilson Carmichael's house on the highest hill in town. The massive house was four-square and solid; three stories with gables, half-dug windows which suggested a full basement, and painted a brilliant white with soft blue trim.

He twisted a bell, and a servant opened the door. The woman wore a stiffly starched uniform of white and black.

"Please tell the master of the house that Sir Malcolm Davies is here to call," Hank said, using a thick British accent. The maid looked up, surprised, closed the door, and hurried away.

A moment later she was back.

"Mr. Carmichael is in the library," the maid said. "He asks you to step this way, please, sir."

The hallway, the stairs, and the rooms opening off were remarkable. No expense had been spared. Hank hadn't seen a house this well furnished and decorated since he left his family plantation in Mississippi.

The library was more of the same, except here it was mahogany paneling, dark oak furniture, and a fireplace with a mantel adorned by several plaques and pictures.

Carmichael sat in a rocking chair and held up a glass of wine.

"Please, Sir Malcolm, join me in a bit of sherry. Just the thing to complete an excellent meal. Oh, I trust you've already dined?"

"Yes, thank you. This house is magnificent. It reminds me of a small castle in York; the same attention to details, the same extraordinary good taste in the decor."

"Well, thank you. We do try to civilize our small part of the Wild West."

"Mr. Carmichael, I've been aware of your tragic loss and the agony you're going through. I'm here to tell you that I've enlisted a group of men, and tomorrow we will go into the foothills in an attempt to find your daughter."

"God bless you, Sir Malcolm. No one else seems to have made a decent try since those two unfortunate men were caught by the Cheyenne."

"Mr. Carmichael, we have some reservations about the participation of the Cheyenne in all of this. So we are going in tomorrow morning with an open mind and with only one purpose: to bring Kitty back into your arms."

"I say Godspeed, Sir Malcolm!"

"The reward, as I remember, was for twenty-five thousand American dollars, am I correct?"

"Yes, that's the figure."

"And this would be in gold, I would expect?"

"If you want gold, you'll have it. A letter of credit, a large stack of greenbacks, however you desire. I just want my little girl!"

"Very good. I just wanted to verify the terms and assure you that our party will do its best."

Hank stood. Carmichael came over and shook his hand.

"The very best tomorrow, Sir Malcolm. We'll be waiting with our hopes high."

Two minutes later Hank was on the street, stepping into his rented coach. He returned it to the livery, paid the two-dollar fee, and hurried back to the hotel. He still had to get his food and gear together for the five-day horseback ride they started in the morning.

Hank got to the general store just before it closed and selected the food and gear he would need to add to his current equipment. He paid for it and said he would pick it up first thing in the morning.

Chapter Nine

QUINN'S RAIDERS gathered at the livery just after eight the next morning. By eight-thirty they had saddled up, mounted, and ridden out of town through a side street and headed west.

There was no real trail. The best route to the far west angled northwest, where it circled around the north end of the Medicine Bow Mountains. While not the highest in the area, some of the Medicine Bow peaks reached over twelve thousand feet, and Elk Mountain at the far north end of the range was more than eleven thousand feet.

With Red Bluff at over seven thousand feet, it still made a hard climb. Most routes simply swung north for forty to sixty miles to go around the chunks of granite and snow-capped peaks, but Quinn and his Raiders headed directly toward the mountains. They were twenty-five miles from town, with the Little Laramie River angling northeast as it dropped out of the foothills and flowed north with the Laramie to eventually join the Platte River, almost a hundred miles north and east.

Loomis rode point in their line of march. He had the best eye—the best nose as well. He could smell a wood fire at five miles, could see a rabbit jump a mile away and sniff out a rancher woman's baked apple pie at twenty miles. At least that's what the other Raiders said he could do.

They rode for two hours and found grassy plains and rolling landscape giving way to some gentle foothills.

They stopped for a talk-out and Marcus pointed due west. "We're between the Laramie River and the Little Laramie. We keep going west, we got to run into it."

They rode again, letting the horses move at a good pace, covering about four miles an hour. From what one old-timer had told Marcus, it ought to have been about eighteen or nineteen miles to the second river from town.

Marcus lifted the mounts to a canter and worked a little faster across the slightly rising ground.

"When them Yanks used to chase us over in Kansas, we could make damn near seven miles an hour," Hank said. He rode over beside Marcus then, wanting to talk.

"You think we're gonna make some money off this little caper?" Hank asked. "I'm starting to run a little short."

"If we find the kid, no reason we shouldn't," Marcus said. "Way I figure it, some owlhoots were in town, heard about Carmichael and his kid, and set up the grab. Then they made it look like Indians to throw off the sheriff."

By noon they could see fringes of green ahead of them as the land had lifted considerably, and they began to work up small valleys and across ridges. Over the second rise they looked down on a wider valley and saw the green swath that a stream created as it worked across the half-desert to the north.

"The Little Laramie," Loomis said. "We can cut

upstream right here and angle over to the water. I think my brother's horse could use a good, long drink pretty soon."

They hit the Little Laramie a half hour later and stepped down to let the horses drink their fill. They all knew a horse working this way needed twenty to thirty gallons of water a day to stay healthy.

The land had changed. Here there was more water, more rain. They had climbed well over a thousand feet from the valley floor and there were now a few Engelmann spruce and ponderosa. Higher up, where there was more rain, there would be the stately Douglas fir. A few aspens and cottonwoods fed on the water from the stream, but the hills were still "dry forest," with almost no underbrush.

"Not a good summer camp place," Bob Depro said. "The Cheyenne probably have six or eight hundred horses, if it's an average-sized band. They need lots of grass for grazing. If they camped here they would overgraze in just a few days and have to move on."

Loomis nodded, a faraway look in his eyes. "These Plains Indians are smart. They wouldn't think of overgrazing around a summer camp. If they did they couldn't come back there toward the end of the summer or next year."

As the horses watered, the Raiders ate. Three of them had brought fresh loaves of bread from the bakery, and now cut off hunks of the bread and spread it with jam from a jar. They added some generous slices of smoked ham. There would be no fire, they all assumed that. The Cheyenne could smell smoke away from their camp for ten miles.

"How far you think we'll need to go before we find them?" Marcus asked, looking at Bob and Loomis.

Loomis shrugged. Bob looked upstream, then at the lay of the hills ahead. "Six, maybe eight miles. No more. Then the canyons get too small, valleys close up, leaving no place for the women to set up the tepees or for the horses to graze."

"We should find a place to leave the horses," Loomis said. "Much easier to slip up on the Cheyenne on foot when we move by night, sleep by day."

"How the hell can we hide five horses up here?" Billy Joe asked.

Bob Depro stood and walked up the side of the stream, which chattered down in a small rapids to the next level, where a small pond had formed. Behind the pond was a sheer rock wall extending up fifty feet. There seemed no reason for it, judging from the other formation of the hundred-yard-wide valley that the Little Laramie had carved down through the centuries.

Bob dropped to his knees and studied tracks in the moist soil along the edge of the twenty-foot-wide stream. He nodded, then trotted upstream. He bent and checked more tracks, then sniffed the air as a dog or a wild animal might.

He walked directly toward a hedge of brush that grew along the base of the sheer rock wall. The water of the stream seemed to course straight for the wall, then bent to the side, where a slab of granite had evidently fallen eons ago, causing the water to take a sharp turn and tumble down to another catch basin twenty vertical feet down a series of rocky rapids.

Bob Depro sat on a rock near the water, watching the tumbling rapids fall across the sheets of granite. He moved to the brush next to the vertical rock slab and looked at the ground again. Slowly he began to nod. His face brightened as he worked along the brush, parting it here and there. At the closest point to the water, he tested the brush again, and in a moment vanished through the stems, branches, and leaves.

"What the hell?" Hank asked. He and the rest of the Raiders had been watching Bob. Now they stood and walked up to the spot where they had last seen him.

His voice came to them clearly. "Come past the brush, it's only a thin screen. Step in here."

Marcus pushed through and found the brush to be less than a foot thick. Beyond it lay a flat, smooth slab of rock that formed the floor of a cave. The opening was only slightly lower than the top of the brush that grew outside. But once into the opening, the roof of the cave rose and the sides expanded into a cavern twenty feet wide, receding into darkness.

On both sides of the cave were coyote droppings and evidence that many animals had used this hidden lair.

"Bring in the horses," Bob said. "We can leave them here. Back a ways is a spot where an underground river surfaces, then sinks back into the sand. Plenty of water for the mounts."

Marcus looked at Bob and thanked him with the glance, then they left to bring back the horses. The first animal was hesitant to walk the narrow ledge of rock and then to enter the brush. Bob took his horse in first, a sensitive little bay mare who seemed to have total trust in Bob.

Bob rubbed the mare's ears, scratched her under the chin, then urged her forward with low sounds in his throat. She nosed into the brush, made a small noise, and walked on through. The other mounts followed her without question.

Bob brought in a twisted, dry weed torch. He lit it with a match and they explored back along the dry walls of the cave for twenty yards until the torch burned out. They found a place to stake the horses near the pool of water.

Back at the front of the cave, they arranged their equipment and caches of food.

"Don't worry about animals eating our supplies," Bob said. "Our man scent is all over here now, and no coyote or bear or fox will come in here for months after we've left."

"We'll take two rifles, whoever wants to carry them, and leave the rest of our gear," Marcus said. "If we don't find the Cheyenne this afternoon or tonight, we'll come back here before it gets light tomorrow."

The five men slipped out through the screen of brush, careful to stay on the rocky ledge along the water so they wouldn't leave any boot prints, and then crossed the shallow stream on the rocks, continuing upstream, which here ran southwest.

Hank and Billy Joe had the rifles. Bob and Loomis led the way along the stream. Now and then they found game trails. Slowly they worked upward, climbing as the stream did. There was more brush now, and here and there the valley opened into mountain meadows a hundred yards wide.

At the edge of one of the open places they saw a half-dozen elk grazing. The five men slipped through the woods in cover and the big animals never even looked up.

"Wind is in our faces," Bob explained. "They never smelled us. They will when we get farther upstream and they'll take off like they were shot."

Another hundred yards upstream, Loomis came to a stop. He held up his hand and then didn't move.

Ahead they heard a bellowing roar. Fifty yards upstream they saw movement. A large black bear ran across a small open place, a year-old cub following ten yards behind her. The she-bear stopped, whirled, and before the cub saw her, she swatted the cub alongside the head, rolling him over three times in the tall grass.

The she-bear stared at the offspring for a minute, then walked away, looking back now and then to be sure the cub wasn't following her. Soon the cub gave up and wandered off in another direction.

Bob Depro grinned. "That's known as being kicked out of the house," he said.

After another half-mile of moving forward, Bob stopped the Raiders. They were at the opening of a valley that looked as if it could be five or six miles long. In places it opened up to nearly half a mile wide. Bob said something to Loomis, who nodded and found a nearby Douglas fir that was close to the edge of the long meadow.

Loomis climbed the tree quickly, moving to the very top of it on the ladderlike branches. When he was so high that the top began to bend under his weight, he stopped and looked up the valley.

He remained there for five minutes, then climbed down.

"So?" Bob asked.

"Might be the place. There are some smokes; ten or fifteen I could make out at the far end of the valley. The trees get thicker up there, lots of spruce and aspens, but it could be the Cheyenne camp."

Marcus looked at Bob. "Should we settle down here and move on up when it gets dark?"

Bob shook his head. "No. What we should do is watch for some Cheyenne hunters. They probably go out in twos and threes. Let's move up a ways along the river and see who we can find."

They walked with caution now. Bob and Loomis flitted from tree to tree, from cover to cover, working upstream half as fast as a man could walk, making sure no one was ahead, beside, or behind them before the next move. They had covered about a mile when Bob froze in place. The others did the same, not moving, hardly breathing. Bob glued himself to the back of a cottonwood. He edged his head to the right and peered past the gray bark.

Marcus could see the movement now. Directly ahead of them, an Indian holding a bow and three arrows in his right hand jogged steadily toward them. His eyes searched the woods on both sides of him, watching for any game he might flush out.

The Indian, wearing a loincloth and moccasins, was a hundred feet in front of Bob Depro. Suddenly a rabbit halfway between the two men darted from cover and ran away from the Indian. The Cheyenne lifted the bow, an arrow already nocked, pulled the bow, and in one fluid motion aimed and fired.

The Cheyenne arrow slanted through the distance and plunged into the side of the rabbit, going all the way through and stumbling the small furry animal to a quick death beside the semblance of a game trail.

Quickly the hunter trotted up to the rabbit and slashed its throat, then, holding it by the hind feet, let the blood drain out of the still-warm body.

As the Cheyenne worked over his kill, Bob and Loomis stalked him silently. Not even a meadowlark interrupted its call from a nearby tree. When they were within six feet of the Cheyenne, both men cocked their revolvers and held them, pointing at the Indian. The Cheyenne looked up at the sound, his eyes going wide.

Quickly Loomis gave the sign for "friend" and "silence." The Cheyenne dropped the rabbit and began to reach for his knife, but by then Bob had jumped to his side and pinned his arms behind him.

The tableau remained that way for a strained twenty seconds, when Loomis Depro began using the Indian words he thought the Plains tribes would understand.

He spoke plainly, slowly, and distinctly, telling the Cheyenne that they were brothers, that they were Indian from the far south, Choctaw, and that they were not there to harm him or any Cheyenne.

Both Depros put their revolvers back in their holsters. They sat on the ground in front of the Cheyenne and released him and asked him to sit and talk.

The Cheyenne warrior used some of the same words the Depros knew, and then began a flood of talk they could not understand.

Again and again they used the words for "friend" and "brother." At last they asked if he could take them to see Hawk's Eye. Loomis remembered the Indian words for the name.

The Cheyenne nodded.

"Now for our surprise," Bob said, turning. "You three white-eyes come on up here, but slowly. One after the other."

As the three white men walked up to the gathering, the Cheyenne showed shock, then pointed at all five of them. Then he used sign language to ask if they all wanted to see Hawk's Eye.

Bob signed to him that they were all friends of the Cheyenne. They all wanted to visit with Hawk's Eye.

The Cheyenne hunter nodded, stood, slung the rabbit over his back, and picked up his bow and arrows. He looked at them all, nodded again, and waved them forward.

They walked through the light growth along the stream toward the far end of the valley.

"What do you think?" Marcus softly asked Bob.

"Not sure, just stay ready. Any damn thing could happen yet. Not sure that he believed our signing."

Ten minutes of walking slowly forward went fine. Then they rounded a bend in the now-beaten trail along the stream, and a wild, shrill scream pierced the soft afternoon silence. Six Cheyenne warriors leaped up, surrounding them, bows all with nocked arrows ready to shoot, and two braves with rifles pointed toward the white men.

Bob Depro looked at the warriors and used the

Indian word for "friend," then signed the word for "friend" and said the name of their chief several times.

The first hunter they caught chattered with the others, but he moved away from where the five Raiders were all standing close to one another, their hands near their weapons.

"Be ready," Loomis said. "This ain't exactly going our way."

Bob signed again and the warriors watched him. He tried to tell them they were hunting for a small white girl about four summers old who was missing.

The first hunter they captured scowled and shook his head, quickly signing that they had no white children in their camp. No white-eye small girl-child.

Bob signed again, hoping that he remembered the right motions. He told them that he was of the People, a Choctaw from far south by the big water. They only wanted to talk to Hawk's Eye, and then they would leave. He said they did not want to settle, to dig in the river, or to cut the trees. They only wanted to make talk with Hawk's Eye.

At last some of the older warriors put down their bows. They talked among themselves. One or two made jokes. The first captive returned to where they stood and talked and signed.

"We understand. Follow us and we will ask Hawk's Eye if he will talk to you."

"Think we just won that one," Marcus said as Bob translated what the hunter had signed.

Then the crisis was over. The Cheyenne were all smiles, came up and looked at the Raiders' weapons, and made a great deal over the two long guns.

It was nearly twenty minutes later when they started walking again toward the far end of the valley, still over three miles away.

The hunter who they first met led the line, followed

by Marcus and his Raiders and the six warriors. They had just come past a thick growth of bushes and vines and moved around a big tree when Marcus heard a roar. It was followed by a bellowing scream.

Marcus rushed ahead with the Raiders to find the first Indian hunter they had met confronted by a huge black bear who had reared up on his back feet and swiped at the Cheyenne with huge front paws.

"Shoot him!" Billy Joe rumbled, lifting his rifle.

"No!" Marcus roared. "Might hit the Cheyenne."

THE OTHER CHEYENNE hunters rushed up, saw the bear, and jumped forward with bows and arrows ready. Bob and Loomis were in front of them, almost on the bear. Bob gave a roar that caught the animal's attention. When the big black head lifted away from the Cheyenne hunter, Bob shot him in the head with his pistol.

The bear hardly noticed it. He swatted the hunter with a huge paw, knocking him down, drawing long bloody claw lines down his shoulder and back.

As soon as the hunter fell away, six arrows sliced into the huge beast's chest and front legs. It bellowed in rage but seemed barely hurt.

Loomis drew his big Bowie knife and ran toward the bear, caught his attention away from the downed Cheyenne hunter, and then darted to one side before the bear could swing a massive paw at him.

Bob darted in from the other side, waving his six-inch hunting knife to distract the bear. Both Depro brothers probed and feinted as if attacking the big bear, drove in, and then jumped out of the way of its slashing claws.

Another volley of Cheyenne arrows pierced the big

bear's chest and throat. He pawed at them as if they
were insect bites.

Hank lifted his rifle and when the Depros were
clear, shot the bear in the throat. The bear wobbled for
a moment, then dropped to all fours and stared at
them. Then the huge black bear roared and lifted up,
proclaiming his dominance over everything and
everybody in the forest.

Loomis ran at the big animal from behind, leaped
on his back, and drove the nine-and-a-half-inch Bowie
knife a half-dozen times into the bear's throat, aiming
to cut a vital artery. The bear spun around, trying to
flip Loomis off. The arrows and the two shots were
starting to make a difference.

The big animal had lost some of its power. Loomis
drove the blade in and ripped it out, then slashed at
the heavy fur and skin on the black bear's neck.

Suddenly a gout of blood surged out of the animal's
throat. Blood gushed out and the bear dropped to all
fours. Loomis vaulted off its back and ran out of range
of its still-deadly claws.

The bear glared at the humans, and swatted at them
even though they were ten feet away. The monster
shook his large, shaggy head and dropped to its
haunches, then his eyes started to glaze and he gave
one more bellowing roar at the attacking Cheyenne.
The hunters sent six arrows into the beast, but again
they seemed to have little effect. The seven-hundred-
pound bear's heart pumped a sea of blood from his
throat onto the thin carpet of the woods floor. He
blinked his eyes, shook his massive head, and then
toppled on its side and lay still.

For a moment there was silence along the chattering
stream in the fringe of woods. Then the high chant of
a shaman shrilled through the woods as the medicine
man called on the spirit of Father Bear to quickly fly

into the heavens while there was still light. He must leave while there was light so his spirit would not be trapped forever in the darkness. When the shaman's cry was complete according to the tradition, then the hunters screamed in delight, dancing around the bear's huge body.

Two of the hunters lifted Loomis on their shoulders and carried him toward the village. One man was left to protect the bear, then they all hurried along the trail, shouting and chanting and treating Loomis as a hero who had made coup many times on the much-feared Father Bear.

Bob grinned at Marcus as they hurried along with the Cheyenne.

"I'm understanding enough of the talk and shouting. The hunters are saying that my little brother is a hero for attacking Father Bear with only his knife. His name will be glorified by the Cheyenne in song and legend for years to come. There will be a special ceremony and a bear feast tonight, and as far as I can tell, Loomis could be elected leader of this band right now if he wants to be."

A runner had rushed ahead to tell the camp about their great victory over Father Bear. By the time the group arrived at the edge of the Cheyenne camp, half the women and children were along the trail, and the warriors had donned their best fighting gear and come to honor the victors.

None of the Raiders had ever been in an Indian village, not even the Depro brothers. They could see many smokes ahead of them. They crossed the stream to the valley side, and soon came to a tepee set up near the water. It was Plains Indian style; a dozen tall poles holding up a cover made of tough winter buffalo hide, carefully stitched together. Now the sides were lifted two feet to allow ventilation through the home.

A warrior rushed out of the tepee and grabbed his shield and bow and lance and ran to the group. He attached himself to the end of the line.

As they worked upstream along a beaten path between the tepees, more and more warriors joined the procession until there were forty of them marching along behind the original group. They carried Loomis to the largest of the tepees and set him down. Then everyone in the entourage quieted and one man stood in front of the big tepee. The Cheyenne were observing the courtesy of waiting for the one inside the tepee to see him and invite him inside or to come out and greet him.

Soon an older Indian left the tepee. He was probably fifty, Marcus decided; old for a Cheyenne. He was slightly bent, but slowly stood up almost straight and looked at his one visitor. They spoke a moment, then the old chief, who Marcus figured was Hawk's Eye, turned and looked at the white men.

He walked forward and stood in front of Loomis Depro. His eyes caught the Indian features, then the white man's clothes and weapons.

He said something sharply and Loomis looked up and nodded, saying two words back and making signs.

The old chief turned and lifted his lance, which had been beside the door of his lodge. He shouted two words, and the whole camp broke into wild cheers.

Bob grinned at Marcus. "Old boy just said let the victory feast of the bear begin. We're gonna have a party."

After Loomis had been congratulated by each of the warriors who came along behind them in the small march through the village, he came over to Marcus.

So far there had been no acknowledgment of the white-eyes in the camp. Loomis sat beside Marcus.

"Hawk's Eye wonders why we white-eyes are here,

but he can't question us during the celebration. It would be bad medicine for him."

"We'll just have to bide our time and watch. I haven't seen any sign of a small white girl around here."

Marcus was fascinated by the Indian camp. The tepees were spaced apart along a quarter-mile of the stream for some privacy, but in no order or pattern. Wherever the woman wanted to put up the tepee, she did.

Most were close to the stream so there would be a shorter distance to carry water. There was no "council fire" area that he had often heard of. Toward the center of the camp there was an open space where no tepees were set up. In the center of it were the remains of a fire, and now Marcus saw women rushing to the fire pit with armloads of wood.

Soon a fire started there and grew.

Six old men with drums came and sat behind the fire. Slowly they began to beat the drums, sometimes alone, sometimes all in unison. Others changed the beat and set up a counterrhythm.

The women scurried around, evidently preparing food. Marcus stood and stretched and walked the length of the camp with Loomis. Nowhere did they see a small white girl. The Cheyenne let them move wherever they wanted to. At the far end of the camp they saw where the band's horses were gathered.

"Five, six hundred mounts!" Marcus said softly.

Loomis smiled. "A Cheyenne is known for the number of horses he owns. Hawk's Eye might own a hundred mounts himself, unless he has given many away. As the leader of this band of Cheyenne, he must be wise but also generous. Anyone in the group can elect to gather his belongings, take his horses, and leave his band anytime."

They wandered back and saw that the feast was progressing. Buffalo robes had been laid out on the grass, and each was piled with food of all kinds: from buffalo jerky to clay bowls of stew to freshly roasted whole rabbits and the specialty—certain parts of the just-killed bear—as well as stacks of cooking bear meat. The delicacies were certain raw parts of the bear, laid out for the warriors who had brought down the bear to eat. None had been sampled yet.

Loomis knew why. The warrior whose life he had saved by taunting the bear walked up stiffly, his shoulder and back covered with large leaves and a poultice of some kind. He chattered a moment and urged Loomis forward.

"Got to do this," Loomis said to Marcus. He went with the Cheyenne over to the buffalo robe where the bear meat and the special parts were laid out. Since he was the honored warrior, it was his right to be the first to partake of the finest part of the bear. There were the bear's eyeballs, his tongue, a pulpy mass of brains, his gonads, and half a dozen other parts, including his heart and liver.

Loomis took his big knife and held it high. Everyone around the camp quieted. He said three words, brought the Bowie down, cut off a slice of the bear's tongue, and ate it.

When he put his knife back in its scabbard down his right leg, there came a roar as the warriors burst forward to claim their favorite parts of the bear's entrails.

Loomis moved out of the way and walked back to where Marcus stood and watched, leaning against a cottonwood tree.

"Tasty?" Marcus asked.

Loomis brushed his hand across his face, and as it came away he held out the slice of raw bear tongue, which he quickly flipped away into the brush. Loomis grinned. "Yeah, real tasty. But I like mine cooked medium rare. I'm more of a white-eye than I sometimes want to admit."

"But still a hero," Marcus teased.

"Hell, I never rode a black bear that big before," Loomis said. "Wanted to give it a try."

The steady beating of the drums increased in speed now. Half a dozen warriors moved onto the hard-packed ground near the drummers and began a slow dance.

Marcus looked at Bob Depro, who had come up. He shrugged.

"Hell, I don't know what's going on. I'm just a quarter-Indian from Dixie. This sure ain't Choctaw doings."

The party was in full flower. The group of Indians here seemed ready to hold a celebration for almost any reason. Now the dance was more complicated. For a while the dancers went all the way around the fire in a large circle, men on the inside, women on the outside, dancing but circling in opposite directions.

Marcus could see no pattern or reason for the particular dance. And they didn't stop.

He looked for some evidence of whiskey, but he saw absolutely none. He knew some of the tribes and Indian bands would have nothing to do with the white man's firewater. This must be one of those.

But they knew no bounds in eating and dancing.

Three hours after sunset, the feasting continued, then suddenly the drums beat furiously for a full minute before going silent.

There was a big cheer from the dancers and eaters, and everyone backed away from the fire and made an avenue. Down the lane came the hunter who had been wounded by the bear. His name was Badger Run. He

rode his war pony, charging in dangerously close to
those waiting for him. He guided the war pony with
his knees only, carrying his war lance in his left hand.
He stopped the pony inches from the crowd, backed it
up, and threw the lance into the ground at the feet of
the drummers. The lance pierced the very edge of the
bearskin, which had been removed from the big black
and brought in quietly for the ceremony.

The injured warrior stood on his war pony's back
and in a loud voice and with many gestures with his
good left hand, he began to harangue the crowd.

Quinn's Raiders had gathered around with Loomis
and Bob and now looked at them curiously.

"That's Badger Run. He's telling the crowd how he
helped kill the bear. He's a local hero now and has his
right to the bear rug. He already asked me if I wanted
it, since he thinks I struck the killing blow. I told him
it was his.

"Now he plays the hero, recounting how brave he
was, how he touched the bear while it was still alive
and counted coup, how he battled the bear until
seriously wounded. This guy should be running for
Congress. He has a fast mouth."

They chuckled and watched the warrior finish his
report, drop off his horse, and send it back down the
row of onlookers. He bent down, caught the edge of
the bearskin, pulled out his lance, and then walked
stiffly back down the opening, dragging the heavy
bearskin with him. Twice he fell. He got up and again
dragged it away to the cheers of the crowd.

Then the dancing resumed. The drums had picked
up the tempo now, and the older dancers gave way to
the younger ones who could keep up the frantic pace.

As they watched the dancers, the wounded Cheyenne who had just claimed his bearskin and all the
honors came up to Loomis. He showed great respect

for Loomis, standing nearby and waiting for Loomis to ask him to talk.

Then he told Loomis his name was Badger Run. He said that Hawk's Eye would see them now. All five walked to the biggest tepee, and the warrior stood beside the lodge and waited. It was ten minutes before Hawk's Eye came to the flap of the tepee and invited them inside.

It was the first time Marcus had been in a tepee. Badger Run showed them inside and motioned for them to walk around the tepee and to stay standing until invited to sit. Loomis quickly told the others what to do.

Hawk's Eye was seated in front of a small fire. When they were in the right position, he chattered to Badger Run, who motioned for them to be seated.

The leader of the Cheyenne band looked at Loomis and in halting English asked: "You wish to speak?"

Loomis did not show surprise at the head man's English. He nodded. "I am Choctaw. Brother. I come in peace."

"Your Cheyenne name, Bear Killer," Hawk's Eye said.

"We come hunting small white-eye girl; four summers."

"We have no white-eye children. We want no war with Pony Soldiers with long guns."

"Good. They want no war, either." Loomis looked at Marcus. "Did your warriors raid a white-eye ranch in the flatlands two days ago?"

Hawk's Eye looked up sharply. He stared at Loomis, then put two more sticks on the fire.

"No raid on flatlands. Last year babies cried in winter. This year we gather much food, kill many buffalo. Start early."

Loomis nodded. "May your hunt be good, your

winters mild, and may your wives have many children."

Hawk's Eye made no move to dismiss them after the traditional Indian parting words. He looked back at Loomis.

"Why ask about flatland raid?"

"Cheyenne arrows, headdress left. Someone tried to make Pony Soldiers think it was the Cheyenne."

"Bad white-eyes do this?"

"We think so, Hawk's Eye."

The band leader stood with difficulty. He held out his hand and shook Loomis's. "White-eye-style thank-you for saving life of Badger Run."

They both nodded shortly and Badger Run led them out of the tepee. Outside they walked a short distance and Billy Joe couldn't keep quiet any longer.

"You see that place? Like a house. A fire in the middle, with smoke goin' through a flap in the top. Sides rolled down with little beds in there and them rawhide boxes filled with some kind of food, and stacks of buff robes?"

"I'll be damned, Billy Joe," Hank said. "Maybe somebody lives in there."

Billy Joe took the teasing and grinned. "We get to go back to the food table again? I saw a half-roasted rabbit down there that I could damn well use."

Badger Run looked at Loomis, who translated, and Badger Run grinned and led the big man back to the food.

An hour later Badger Run came to them with five buffalo robes. Loomis found out they were asked to sleep in an area near the big tepee, so everyone would know where they were and not mistake them in the night for white-eyes attacking the village.

When they rolled on the buffalo robes, the white men were surprised how soft the hair was.

"Like a damn fur coat," Bob said. He laughed.

"Hell, us Choctaw didn't have no buffalo in Mississippi."

Marcus lay there listening to the last of the dancers and the slower beating of the drums. Loomis said the drums would continue until the last dancer dropped from exhaustion.

Chapter Eleven

LOOMIS SAGGED ONTO his buffalo robe and looked at the stars through the high-country mountain sky. He swore the stars were much closer to earth up here than in Mississippi. He grinned. At least seven or eight thousand feet closer.

Someone approached and he sat up on the robe. The others were sleeping. The figure came silently, but without stealth. It was Badger Run.

Badger Run motioned for Loomis to follow him. When they were well away from the others, Badger Run smiled at Loomis in the moonlight.

"A favor I ask of you," Badger Run said with signs and the few words they both knew.

Loomis lifted his brows, wondering what it might be, but he nodded. They walked past a dozen tepees, then stopped at one where Badger Run led the way inside. A bright fire burned in the fire pit, and Loomis could see several sleeping beds around the walls.

Loomis noticed lumps under light robes on two of the beds. Badger Run stopped at the third one, farthest back from the fire. He sat down on the edge of the poles and the buffalo-skin bed. With a start, Loomis saw someone in the bed.

Badger Run touched Loomis's shoulder. He motioned at the person in the bed. "My number-three wife, the youngest. She has only sixteen summers. You sleep here tonight."

In one moment, Loomis realized what this man had done. He offered one of his wives to him for the night to somehow make up for what Loomis had done for him that day. Loomis could remember his mother talking about the practice of loaning wives. Even the Choctaw had no problem with that. Especially if a man was a little older and could not sire a son. It was perfectly acceptable in some tribes as long as it was the husband's idea.

Loomis started to shake his head, then he remembered what his mother had told him. To refuse such an offer would be a terrible insult to an Indian warrior.

He looked at the bed and now saw the young girl sit up. Even in the soft light he could see that she wore nothing. She was slender and her face was strong and pretty. She held out a hand to him.

Loomis looked back at Badger Run, but already the warrior had slipped away, a smile on his face. Oh, damn! Loomis thought. There was no way that he could refuse the gift. She would be expecting it, he couldn't just lie beside her. The girl moved closer to him and pulled at the strange clothes he wore. She opened his blue cotton shirt and rubbed his chest, then she caught his hands and pulled them to her bare, warm breasts. She was exactly what Loomis liked in a girl; young and eager for lovemaking. Her breasts were so soft, her small nipples were hard, and he felt them pulsing excitedly.

She murmured something and stripped off his shirt. Quickly he pulled off his boots and pants and slid onto the buffalo robe beside her.

Somewhere ahead of them, an older woman's voice

chattered a half-dozen words that Loomis couldn't understand, and Badger Run shushed her.

Loomis let his hands run down the young girl's torso and soon knew she was wearing nothing at all. He pulled off his short underwear, and she gave a little cry when she rolled on top of him.

Loomis grinned in the dark. She might be young, but she knew exactly what to do to satisfy a man. He let her take the lead and knew it was going to be an extremely long and exhausting night.

He grinned and found her breasts again. It had been a long time for him.

The next morning, Marcus had been concerned when he found Loomis not sleeping near the other Raiders. Bob laughed softly. "Don't worry about little brother. Just about when everyone got to sleep, Badger Run came for him. I'd bet half my pair of six-guns that the young man had himself the loan of one of Badger Run's wives last night."

Hank Proudy looked up quickly.

"You mean they do that? Badger Run was so thankful for having his life saved that he pushed Loomis into bed with his wife?"

"Probably. We'll ask him. Badger Run must have at least two women."

Badger Run came up to them shortly after and motioned for them to come for a morning meal. They had a kind of stew and some tough buffalo jerky. He brought the food to them just outside of his tepee. Loomis sat there whittling on a stick. He was working on a small whistle made out of a hollow stick.

Bob grinned at Loomis. "Hey there, youngster, you look plumb tuckered out this morning."

"Don't you know it ain't right to laugh about such an unselfish act?" Loomis said. Then he grinned himself. "It was just fine . . . mighty fine. Now let's eat."

Marcus had trouble with the stew, especially when Bob found out from Badger Run that the meat in it was either possum, squirrel, or timber rat.

During the meal, Marcus got together with Loomis and Badger Run.

"Ask him if there have been any reports of white-eyes anywhere in this area, or even out toward the big plains. We're hunting some white-eyes who must have kidnapped the little girl."

It took Loomis some time to get across the idea to Badger Run. He shook his head, then said something and hurried away.

"He said he hadn't seen any. He'll ask the other warriors and their long-range hunters if they have seen anyone."

The Raiders finished their food, all of it as Loomis reminded them, and were throwing rocks into the stream when Badger Run came back nearly an hour later. His eyes glowed as he talked with Loomis.

After several minutes of signing and a word here and there, Loomis nodded.

"Badger Run says one of the long-range hunters looking for elk saw one white-eye along the river. He was high up, and by the time he got close to him, the white-eye hurried away."

"Ask him if the warrior can take us to the spot."

He could.

An hour later the five Raiders, Badger Run, and a hunter-warrior called Bold Elk stood along the Little Laramie River well down from the big valley, but three or four miles above the cave where their horses waited.

Bold Elk showed the men where he had seen the white-eye.

109

"What was he doing?" Loomis asked Badger Run.

"Bold Elk says he was playing in the water with metal pans."

"Panning for gold," Hank said. Hank moved over to the edge of the stream and reached down into a riffle where sand had piled up in six inches of water behind a rock. He scooped up the sand and lifted it out of the water.

Even as the water drained away they all could see the specks and flakes of bright yellow gold.

"My God!" Marcus said. "Now we know why somebody has been trying to get these Cheyenne into trouble. Somebody knows this is a prime panning area, which means there's another mother lode around here somewhere. Who would be most interested in knowing about that?"

"Could be Carmichael," Hank said. "He could have staged the kidnapping of his own daughter, let the women come through, but made certain his hired hands killed the men."

"Then they follow up with supposedly 'Cheyenne' problems," Marcus said. "All of them could be pulled off by four or five men with good rifles and a few Cheyenne arrows, lances, and feathered head gear."

"If Carmichael is behind it, he sure as hell won't pay no twenty-five thousand to get his little girl back," Billy Joe said. "He knows where she is."

"If we bring her in, the bastard will pay, even if he set up the kidnapping," Marcus said, his voice cold, deadly. "Even if we have to take every dollar out of his hide."

"Looks like we got us some hunting to do, boys," Hank said. "Some white sidewinders, cousins to cottonmouths."

Marcus nodded. "Next, we'll talk with our Cheyenne hosts to find out if they know about any old trapper cabins or mountain men log cabins between where they are and Red Bluff. Been mountain men up in this area for fifty years. Bound to be some hidden cabins or caves around here somewhere."

That afternoon, Marcus and Loomis spent an hour toasting in the sun with Hawk's Eye, and four of the older warriors who knew the land between the two Laramie rivers.

Once Loomis got the idea across to the five warriors, with the help of Badger Run, the old men chattered among themselves and drew maps in the dirt. It took them nearly an hour to agree, but at last they had decided upon something.

"There seems to be some confusion," Loomis reported. "But they do remember three strong cabins that the mountain men built. They're probably still standing since they cut down logs over two feet thick to build the walls, stacking the logs on top of each other and holding them together with notches."

Loomis brought Marcus to the map drawn in the dirt.

"Here's the Laramie River, and the town's about here." Loomis pointed but did not disturb the map. "Over here is the Little Laramie where it comes down out of the hills. In between there are three major ridgelines running down to the plains of No Elk.

"On the second ridge, near some small feeder waters, they think there are two cabins, built well, but not seen for many years. This is because they are within half a day's ride of the town of the white-eyes, and Cheyenne wish to stay farther away from the firewater town than that."

The briefing was over. Hawk's Eye was told about the white-eyes who had been panning for gold. He indicated that the squaw clay was good only for making trinkets.

"White-eyes will kill for the squaw clay," Marcus said. "They would tear up the valley, dig up the river, dig into the mountains."

That evening Quinn's Raiders ate with Badger Run's family again. This time they had a massive chunk of bear roast that had been cooking over a large open fire since the day before. It was slightly charred on the outside, but inside the eight-inch slab of bear meat it was so tender and juicy and well done that they ate until they could hold no more.

The three wives of Badger Run laughed about how much Billy Joe ate. They stared up at him when he stood. None of them had ever seen a human being so big before, not even the two or three white-eyes they had seen before from a distance were this big.

That night the Raiders hit their blankets early. They would move out in the morning to hunt the cabins, or a newer cabin that had been built just for the use of the kidnappers.

Badger Run knew the white-eyes would be leaving in the morning. He touched Loomis on the shoulder and said that he expected Loomis to be his guest in the tepee again that night. Loomis nodded. "A warrior's duty," he mumbled, smiling.

That night Small Flower waited for him and murmured in delight when he slid into her bed. The softness of her delicious young body pressed against him, anxious to see how many times this part-Indian, part–white-eye could make love to her.

Somewhere during the evening or the very early morning hours, Loomis and Small Flower lost count.

The next morning, when Quinn's Raiders got ready to leave from the Cheyenne camp, Badger Run insisted that they eat first. He had more bear for them, this time slabs of the bear meat cut into steaks and cooked over a slow fire. It was the last day the bear meat would be good, even though they had sunk a big slab in the creek to keep it cool.

The steaks were not as good as the roast the night before, but they ate, dutifully, and Billy Joe asked for a second piece. As they assembled to move out, Badger Run brought a special gift to Loomis; a traveling buffalo robe.

He explained that it was from a late-fall calf which had hair so soft and fine that it felt like a fox fur. It was only about three feet square and had been folded up in a small package, tied with rawhide strips of buffalo hide.

Loomis knew he must make a return gift and thought of his big Bowie knife, but couldn't part with it. He then remembered his pocket knife. He pulled it out, showed Badger Run how to open and close all three blades, and made it a present. Badger Run received it with respect.

An hour later, Quinn's Raiders arrived at their secret cave and slipped inside. The horses were still there, nervous and hungry but well watered. The men put on the saddles, loaded up their gear, and walked the animals out through the screen of brush. At the first good graze they stopped for a half hour and let the animals take on some nourishment.

After another watering they headed back toward the Laramie River.

By noon they had climbed over the first ridge, and it was getting close to nightfall when they had worked their way nearly to the top of the second ridge. Somewhere to the north, downhill, they should find one of the old cabins that had been built at least twenty years before by some wandering mountain men.

Smoke would be their best beacon. Even a hidden smoke—a cabin set in a deep cover of trees to absorb and scatter the smoke as it came out—could not all be hidden. The hardly visible, pungent wisps of wood smoke would ride the air currents for miles and trigger a sensitive nose.

Marcus sat on his horse and stared out over the miles of well-timbered slopes starting at their feet, and then at the thinning timber that went all the way down to the grasslands. Somewhere out there in about a hundred square miles was the small child.

He put Loomis and Depro in the lead, and they headed downhill into the light breeze, hoping for a lucky smoke.

QUINN'S RAIDERS WERE less than a mile down the long second ridge from the Medicine Bow when Bob Depro stopped short. He lifted his head and sniffed the air, turned his face from side to side, and sniffed again.

"Smoke," he said. "Not close, but wood smoke. We might be on the right track."

They were in heavy cover and worked down the side of the ridge slowly. Bob moved them across to the east side of the ridge and nodded. The smoke smell was getting stronger.

Looking ahead, the Raiders could see that the timber started to thin. There were mostly ponderosa pines and a few Engelmann spruce.

At the next deep cover, Bob stepped down from his mount, and the rest did so as well.

"Better leave the horses here and let Loomis and me work on ahead to see what we can find. Too many boots gonna spook somebody down there. Might be a mile, might be two. Wherever it is, the old cabin will be in one of those heavy-growth spots. No wonder the place has lasted so long."

The Depros tied their horses and worked down the

slope. They had only their revolvers and knives. It was a scouting expedition.

Bob and Loomis flowed down the side of the ridge like a pair of shadows, drifting from one cover to another, moving with ease. They took their time to keep from attracting the eye of any casual observer.

In the second heavy growth of timber and brush, a half mile from where they had left the horses, the brothers paused, looking out over the next stretch of sparse growth.

"Smoke isn't any stronger here than it was above," Loomis said.

Bob nodded. "Damn strange."

"Could have blown in from five miles away."

"Let's try another two hundred yards, then we'll bring up the horses."

They worked down the slope again, staying well up on the side of the ridge. The next heavier growth came in a ribbon that extended down the slope in a gentle sweep, as if some forester had replanted it years ago.

They worked through it, then on a hunch followed the swath of timber down almost to the edge of the valley below.

Bob touched Loomis's shoulder when they came out of some heavy brush. He pointed ahead.

The back of an old log cabin showed through some of the brush and timber. The two Choctaws melted back into the cover and stared at the structure.

"Damn old," Bob said. They began working around the cabin, staying well out of sight in the cover. It took them a half hour to get to where they could see the front of it.

"No smoke from the stone chimney," Loomis said.

"Fire could have gone out. That's why we didn't get any stronger smoke smell."

They edged closer. There was a high window on one

side but no glass in the empty black square. The front door now sagged by the top hinge. As they watched, a small red fox stepped through an opening at the bottom of the tilted door. The fox paused, looked directly at where the two men crouched out of sight, twitched its nose, ears stiffly alert, then it darted to the left and into the brush.

"Let's take a look, anyway," Bob said. It was obvious that no humans were in the log cabin or had been recently.

They ran to the door and pushed it aside. The log cabin was still sturdy. The eighteen-inch logs on the base, tapering up to twelve inches at the top of the walls, would last another hundred years.

Inside it was musty and dusty. Trailing vines had grown through the door and along the hard-packed floor. There was a fireplace, a small table, and one chair made of limbs and rawhide. A pole-and-hide bed stood in one corner. On one shelf sat a tin of something that had lost its label to bugs and snails.

On the table lay an old flintlock pistol. A half-dozen balls and something that could have been powder lay near it in a small pile. There was no skeleton, no bones. Foxes, coyotes, maybe a small bear had made a nest at one time or another inside the man-made shelter.

Outside they paused. "I'll go back and get the others," Loomis said.

Bob nodded. "I'll scout on ahead and then meet you back here in half an hour or so."

Loomis turned and jogged up the hill, working silently from habit. He would cover the mile and a half back to the horses in about fifteen minutes, even working up the hill and along the slope of the ridge.

It was almost an hour later when they all met just below the old cabin. Billy Joe grabbed the flintlock pistol and checked it over. It was intact, and with some oiling and minor repairs he could make it function again.

They found little else of value in the cabin.

"Might not have been used for twenty years," Marcus said.

When Bob came back from his scout, he shook his head.

"Lost the smoke scent, worked down half a mile and found nothing."

He and Marcus went out to the edge of the heavy timber, where they could see the land falling away toward the grasslands far below.

"How far down do you think we should check this ridge?" Marcus asked.

"Another four or five miles. Then the cover won't be thick enough to hide a cabin," Bob said. "Might as well stay mounted until we see something."

They worked down the slopes again on their horses.

It was nearly five that afternoon and still they had come up empty. There had been no more sign of the wood smoke they had smelled earlier.

"Might as well find a spot with some water and hole up for the night," Marcus said.

They were so far down the ridge that they had run out of heavy cover, so they worked their way back up along a trickle of water to some Engelmann spruce and a copse of cottonwoods and made camp. Marcus decided they might as well have a cooking fire if anyone wanted one.

"These white-eyes we're hunting probably couldn't smell wood smoke if it was blown up their noses," Bob said.

"We'll be moving with daylight," Marcus told them. "Best bet'll be to head over to the next ridge and start working back up it."

"We lost the wind for showing us a smoke," Bob said. "Most of the wind here will be at our backs, moving in that direction."

"Have to make do," Marcus said.

Morning dawned bright and cloudless. A meadowlark called them out of their blankets. They took time for breakfast so that they could have a free fire and eat up some more of their soft foods.

For an hour they worked up the next ridge. They were now within ten or twelve miles of Red Bluff. Too damn close, Marcus figured, for any kind of a hideout.

By nine-thirty the wind had changed. Loomis looked at the sky and saw some high strata clouds blowing in over the basin. Far to the west they could see a front of dark clouds moving slowly.

"Could be some rain this afternoon," Loomis said.

Bob started to grin. "Soon it will be time to stash the horses somewhere," he said. "Damn strong smoke coming downwind. I'd guess half a mile at the most."

All five moved up the side of the big ridge. Bob shifted them to the east side and nodded. Now they all could smell the smoke.

"Damn, I got a whiff of frying bacon," Billy Joe grunted.

"You just smelled your own beard," Hank teased.

Slowly they moved up the slope along the side of the ridge. The cover was adequate here, and all knew that if they found a second cabin it would be three hundred yards downslope, near the small stream they could see below.

Bob and Loomis led the patrol slowly forward. The cover was strong enough for them to move the horses at a slow walk. They went past an area where another swatch of ponderosa swept down from the ridge to the valley. It was over a quarter of a mile wide and as they

119

came out on the far side of it, they could look a half-mile up the small valley below.

"Yeah!" Bob Depro said. He pointed and they could see smoke filtering up through a dense growth of pines and cottonwoods at the base of the ridge where the tiny stream had vanished.

"Got them," Marcus said.

Now, making sure of their cover, they moved to the far side of the ridge and rode up a mile, then crossed the ridge and spotted the smoke again. Stealthily, they worked downslope through the pine and Douglas fir toward the faint beginnings of the tiny trickle of water.

They found a brushy spot and left their horses. Bob led the probe toward the cabin which they knew must be there. Each man had his pistol and favorite second weapon handy. Billy Joe carried his big Mare's Leg .58-caliber Springfield pistol-carbine. Hank had his sawed-off Greener ten-gauge shotgun, and Bob his bullwhip.

Bob moved slowly on the point. He made certain not to step on a dry twig, or let a branch swish behind him as he passed it. Fifteen minutes slipped by as they moved a hundred yards. The wind had shifted again, blowing the smoke back toward them.

Marcus had said there would be no shooting until they had found little Kitty and took her out of danger.

The timber thinned a little. Now the only trees remaining were the tougher ponderosa pines, the Engelmann spruce, and cottonwoods. Wherever there was a taste of water in Wyoming, there would be cottonwoods in the lower elevations.

After another half hour of working silently forward, they could see the cabin. It was old and sturdy, made of notched logs. They came at it from the back and could see no window. Bob made a solo scout to the left and came back saying there was no window on that side. Loomis checked the right and found none, either.

They pulled back fifty yards and made a sweeping arc to the left through the heavier timber and brush so that they could see the front of the place.

The corral showed first. Three horses stood in an old pole corral that had half fallen down. Bob whispered with Marcus, then moved forward. The corral could not be seen from the cabin unless someone came outside.

It was a few minutes past noon. The smoke kept coming from the cabin. Bob eased up to the corral and talked softly to the three horses. They were not alarmed. Bob had a way with animals, horses especially. One little mare came over to him and nuzzled his hand.

Bob used his rifle stock to pry one of the poles off the post. He swung it down quietly. The middle pole had rotted and fallen away. Bob stepped on the bottom pole and it fell apart with hardly a sound. One by one, Bob led the horses out of the corral. Loomis was there to take two of the mounts by the bridles, leading them deep into the forest cover, where he tied them.

The Raiders then moved on around so they could see the front of the cabin.

As they watched, one white man came out and headed for a caved-in outhouse. He was a big man, well over six feet. He walked behind the outhouse, dropped his pants, and squatted.

Loomis Depro pointed at him and Marcus nodded. Loomis slid through the brush silently, jumped the small waterway, and came up behind the big man just as he started to pull up his pants. Loomis ran and dove at the man, hitting him in the back and driving him to the ground.

Loomis had his big knife out and now he held it by

the blade and slammed the heavy handle down on the
white man's skull. The man lifted one hand, but then
sighed and lost consciousness.

Running out to help Loomis, Billy Joe lifted the
bulk on his shoulder and carried him back in the
woods fifty yards, dumped him on the ground, and
slapped his face until he came to. Loomis had already
tied his hands and feet with strips of rawhide he
always carried.

"What the hell?" the man said, shook his head, and
blinked.

He saw the big Bowie-knife blade at his throat and
looked up at Loomis.

"Keep it quiet or you're a dead man, understand?"
Loomis growled at him.

The man nodded.

"How many men inside?"

"Two more. Slade, he's gone to Red Bluff to find out
what's happening."

Marcus and Bob slipped up beside them. Marcus
heard the answer. It was open, naive; a little simple,
perhaps.

"Is the little girl Kitty all right?" Marcus asked.

"'Course. She's fine. Eats good. Got to keep her
healthy so we can get the ransom."

"You help kidnap her?" Marcus asked.

"Sure, it was easy. They didn't expect us . . .
Indians." He looked up at the four of them. "You . . .
you guys working with us?"

"Might be. You work for Mr. Carmichael?"

"Carmichael . . . Same name as the little girl, Kitty.
Work for her father? No. We work for Slade. The three
of us. He hired us in Red Bluff in a saloon. If you're
with us, why did you knock me down and hurt me?"

"We're not with you or with Slade," Marcus said.
"What's your name?"

"Possum."

"Somebody coming up the trail," Hank said.

"Take him quietly," Marcus said. "We don't want to tip off the other two inside."

Bob and Hank took off running through the cover. They went downstream and saw a man riding a horse up the faint, brush-filled path into the cabin. He was still a hundred yards away.

Bob shook out the bullwhip and found a small open spot where he could use it. He nodded and stepped behind a big cottonwood trunk. Hank ran on down the trail and faded behind a giant ponderosa pine. He had out a knife. His scatter gun hanging by its cord around his neck wouldn't help here.

The rider came on the horse at a walk. He was grinning, and Hank wondered why. Hank let the rider slip past him, circling the tree trunk to stay out of sight. He shadowed the rider, staying close behind.

When the rider entered the small clearing where Bob hid, Hank let out a small cry and ran at Slade. At the same time Bob stepped out and saw Slade look behind him. Depro's bullwhip snaked out and caught Slade's right hand.

Bob jerked backward with all of his weight and yanked Slade off the horse. Slade cried out, but before he could do anything more he hit the dirt hard, and Hank dove on his back, grinding him into the ground.

Hank's knife drove forward, catching the kidnapper in the side. He twisted the blade and ripped it out. Slade groaned and held his side and belly where the blade had sliced out.

He looked up and sighed. "You done killed me!" Slade said, then his eyes went dull, a last gush of air came out of his lungs, and his bladder emptied.

Bob Depro came up, unwrapped the thin end of the

bullwhip from the dead man's arm, and coiled it. Then he caught the horse, which had started grazing, and led it deep into the woods.

Hank picked Slade up by the feet and pulled him into the brush. Then they went back to where Marcus held Possum sitting against a tree. They had learned all they wanted from him, and now his own neckerchief bit through his open mouth as a gag.

"The one he called Slade done paid in full measure for the plantation," Bob said.

Marcus nodded. "Two down. Two inside. No windows in that place. Some old mountain man played it real safe."

"The other two'll come out to the convenience sooner or later," Hank said.

"What?" Billy Joe asked.

"The shitter over there," Loomis interpreted.

"We could walk up to the door, kick it open, and surprise them, covering both of them," Hank suggested.

"Might work, but one of them might get a shot off at the girl."

"Pretty soon they gonna be wondering where Possum here went," Billy Joe said.

Marcus took out a paper and a stub of a pencil. He went to Possum. "Can you write?"

The big man nodded. "Write down the names of the two men inside, or Loomis here will cut you a new windpipe."

Possum seemed to have finally realized that these men were not his friends. He shook his head. His eyes widened as he felt the big knife at his neck, and as he shook his head he cut himself on the stationary blade. It wasn't a deep cut, but blood ran down his throat.

Marcus wet his fingers with it and held them up so Possum could see his own blood.

"How much of this red stuff do you think you can

lose and still stand trial, Possum?"

The man's eyes widened and he reached for the pencil. On the pad of paper, he printed in block letters the names Dirk and Flinch.

"Thanks, Possum. You might just have saved your skin."

Marcus looked at the big man, saw he was tied again, then worked his way silently back to where he could see the front of the cabin through the brushy cover.

It was a long shot, but a chance he had to take. Marcus stood still and motioned for Hank to come with him.

Marcus talked to Hank a minute, telling him what they were going to do. Both men grinned.

MARCUS AND HANK would have to walk up and open the door. Those inside would assume it was Possum coming back. With any luck, the two would be separated and away from Kitty.

"Don't blow them away unless we have to," Marcus said. "We should take them easy."

As he said, it did sound easy. Side by side they stood outside the door, so they both could burst through the door at the same time.

Hank unsnapped the scatter gun and held it hip high, aimed inward. Marcus pointed his six-gun the same direction.

Marcus nodded. Hank in front unlatched the doorknob and kicked the door inward.

They jumped into the room. The two men were waiting for them. Marcus and Hank took in the situation in a hundredth of a second. One man was moving from an upturned table across to a pair of turned-over chairs. He lifted his revolver as he dove for the chairs.

The ten gauge blasted one round of double-aught buck. The sixteen slugs, the size of a .32 round, caught the man in the air and blew him backward against the fireplace, where one leg and foot flopped into the burning fire. The slugs nearly cut his torso in half, and he died before he hit the wall.

The second man rose from behind the table and fired just as Marcus blasted a round over the top, as he would on general principle. Both rounds missed flesh. Hank and Marcus dove in opposite directions as the kidnapper behind the table fired three more times.

When the noise died down and the blue smoke began to settle, the man behind the table called to them.

"I got me an ace in the hole," the kidnapper said.

"What's that?" Marcus asked.

"Small girl, four or five. Name's Kitty. I've got my weapon against the side of her head. You two lay down your weapons and let us walk out of here, or I blow her into hell!"

"Easy for you to try, but then you die, too," Marcus said.

"No, not a chance. You come for the kid. You won't risk getting her hurt. She's hurt, you get no damn reward."

Marcus had rolled behind a makeshift bed and Hank lay on the floor, fully exposed but with the shotgun up and ready with the second barrel.

It was quiet in the cabin for fifteen or twenty seconds, then the little girl sobbed.

"That man's foot is on fire," Kitty said.

Marcus saw the dead man's foot hanging in the fire. His pant leg was burning. There was nothing they could do about it.

"You ready to parley?" the kidnapper asked.

"We ain't going nowhere," Marcus said.

"Look, I didn't like this latch-up from the gitgo. Tell you what. I carry the brat out the door and into the woods. You don't shoot at me and I don't kill her. I get to the woods and out of sight, and I let the kid go and you can have her. This ain't worth me dying for."

"Your best offer?" Marcus asked.

"Damn right, and you got no choice. I'm moving out now. I can't shoot you, or I'd have to move the gun off the kid. You can't shoot me, or I'll blow her brains out. Kind of a Cheyenne standoff. Don't go getting fast on the trigger now."

The man lifted up slowly, saw Hank, and then Marcus.

"Hold steady now, just hang on and nobody else gets killed. I didn't even know Flinch there good. Hell, he's no grit outta my craw." The kidnapper moved as he talked. He came up in the open, Kitty Carmichael held tightly around the waist, his six-gun muzzle against her head. He moved slowly, walking toward the door.

"Know my back's gonna look inviting, but you blow me away, I pull the trigger reflex action, and the kid is blood and brains all over. Understand?"

He was halfway across the room, six feet from the door.

"Yeah, we hear you," Marcus said. "We ain't shooting. Just be sure you let go of the girl when you get to the brush. We can't hurt you none from way in here."

"Way I figure, I got no bitch with you two. You win this one, and I lose. Don't try to track me, you'll never find me in this brush." He was out the door then. He closed it behind him and they heard him running.

Marcus came to his feet and raced to the door. He pushed it open a crack so they could see. The man looked around the empty yard, then walked quickly toward the brush.

"Hope Billy Joe stays out of sight," Marcus said.

"Soon as they heard those shots they'd either be up on the walls or well hidden to see who came out," Bob said.

The kidnapper got to the woods, moved back into

the brush, and angled for a cottonwood. There he put the little girl down and jumped behind the tree trunk, pulling the weapon away from her head at the last moment.

Kitty sat down in the leaves and cried.

That was the only sound for two minutes, then a rifle snarled farther down in the woods.

"Should be it," Marcus said. They walked out and picked up the little girl. She stared at them. She was clean, her face and hands were washed, and her dress was dusty but not dirty, even after five or six days.

Marcus held her. "Kitty, my name is Marcus, and we're going to take you back to your folks. Will you like that?"

She nodded.

Loomis came out of the woods twenty yards down from them. He carried his rifle and looked at Marcus, then nodded.

"Shot that rattlesnake I been hunting," he said. He paused for a minute. "Guess I should go get the horses rounded up. No sense letting three good mounts go to waste out here in the wilderness."

Hank and Billy Joe brought up their five horses, and everyone got ready to move. Marcus used a folded blanket to make a softer pad for Kitty to ride on in front of him. Possum would be taken back for the sheriff.

Bob tied the three kidnappers' mounts on a lead line string and settled down each horse, then they started the trip back to town. They were no more than a mile from the cabin when they saw movement ahead and settled back into some brush and watched.

A cavalry patrol moved into the timbered section of the ridgeline.

"Heading across this one, moving deeper toward Hawk's Eye," Loomis said.

"No sense in letting them see us," Marcus said. "We'll wait a half hour. By then they should be over the ridge and out of sight."

Bob Depro rode out as scout to watch the Pony Soldiers. He came back with the word that they were moving toward the third ridge.

Quinn's Raiders rode down the first ridge toward Red Bluff. It was little more than a two-hour ride from where they were. They would be back in town well before dark.

"We're taking you home," Marcus told Kitty. She turned and looked at him and smiled.

They made a strange little caravan as they rode into the outskirts of town two and a half hours later: the five Quinn's Raiders in their long dusters and black hats, the one man tied to the saddle horn, and a string of three riderless horses following behind.

By the time they stopped at the sheriff's office, there were twenty young boys and old men following them.

"That the Carmichael kid?" one toothless old man called.

Nobody answered him.

Sheriff Markowski saw them coming and hurried out.

"Found her, by God!" he yelped.

Marcus nodded. "True, and here is the surviving kidnapper. Gent by the name of Slade engineered it all. He and Dirk and Flinch went down in combat. This gent's name is Possum. Had been in town for a while. He's a little slow witted, so I don't know what you'll want to do with him."

"We'll take care of it. You best get up to the Carmichael house. I'll show you where it is."

The sheriff mounted up and rode with them.

Mrs. Carmichael came running out of the big house when they rode up near the front door. Tears streamed down her face. She couldn't speak. She lifted her baby off the saddle and hugged her and hurried back into the house.

"Overcome," the sheriff said. "I'm your witness if you need any with Carmichael. He's out to the mine today. Should be back about six. He'll be finding you at the hotel. Now, I better get back to the prisoner." He rode off.

At the livery they unsaddled their horses, and Bob Depro bargained with the livery owner about buying the three extra mounts.

"Three fine animals," Bob said. "Worth at least forty dollars each, and another twenty for the saddles."

"Give you thirty and fifteen. Hell, I got to make some profit."

Bob shrugged and took the $135 and walked back to the hotel with the rest of them. The Raiders split the money.

Hank headed for a bath and some clean town clothes.

Billy Joe had missed dinner, so he combed his beard and stormed into the Grasslands Cafe for some food.

Bob and Loomis Depro went up to their room to try out the beds.

Marcus washed up in the basin in his room and wondered if Carmichael would really come up with the $25,000. His share was almost enough to retire on, buy a little spread somewhere, and raise blooded horses.

He put on clean clothes and checked his key box in the lobby. There were three messages, all in sealed envelopes. He took them and sat in the lobby and read them.

Each was from Agnes Ballard, the schoolteacher. Each said, "Come see me when you get back." Marcus allowed he would, as soon as he could after it got dark.

Marcus was heading for the cafe when someone called to him. He turned slowly and found H. Wilson Carmichael heading toward him.

"You find that Englisher for me? Understand you was with him when he brought back my Kitty."

"I was. You got the money?"

"Of course. Where's the Englisher?"

"Probably in the Elk Horn Saloon," Marcus said. "Right this way." They went into the saloon and found Hank out of his bath and already into a poker game.

"Englisher! You did it, by damn!" Carmichael shouted.

Hank stood and used his accent. "Ah, Mr. Carmichael. I'd say you have brought us something?"

"Yes, indeed, and I'm right proud to do so." He reached in a small case he carried and lifted out a stack of bills. "Here is your reward, five thousand dollars in cash, just as I promised."

A murmur went through the crowd.

Hank looked up sharply. "No!" he said loudly. "The public notice of reward was twenty-five thousand dollars. You're a wee bit short there, Mr. Carmichael."

"Not true at all," Carmichael said, looking surprised. "The sum was five thousand. Isn't that right, Sheriff Markowski?"

"Indeed, it is, Mr. Carmichael. That's the figure you told me, that's the figure on the notice in writing you gave me, and that's the figure you announced at the public meeting."

Hank bristled. "Ask anybody who don't work for the mine. You'll see it's really twenty-five. You still owe me and my men twenty thousand, Mr. Carmichael. I hope that will weigh heavy on your conscience."

132

Marcus pushed up beside the lawman. "You buy cheap, don't you, Sheriff?" Billy Joe had come in while the talk went on. Marcus nodded at him and Hank and they walked out of the saloon.

"The bastard!" Hank exploded when they were outside. "I went and talked to him before we left, and he guaranteed me twenty-five thousand."

"He's a man close with his money," Marcus said. "He figures he can save twenty thousand and run us out of town."

"His mistake," Hank said.

"His damn big mistake," Marcus echoed. "That potbellied man with almost no hair is going to pay us in cash, whether he likes it or not."

They walked down the street and found Loomis and Bob heading for supper at the cafe. They talked in hushed tones.

"What does the bastard have that we can collect on?" Marcus asked.

"His mine," Bob said.

"The payroll," Hank said. "What did you figure that cash payroll would run for a month?"

"About ten thousand. It gets a military escort usually of ten cavalry troopers since it goes through Cheyenne territory."

"That ten thousand will be no trouble," Billy Joe said. "What else has he got? He still owes us another ten thousand."

"The bank," Marcus said. "I found out he owns the bank and keeps some of his money there. There should be ten thousand in cash there."

"We'll make a withdrawal," Loomis said. "A night withdrawal, and leave a paper telling them who to charge it to."

They all grinned.

"When?" Hank asked.

"When is the payroll due?" Loomis asked. "No sense our hitting the bank, then waiting a week out in the woods when we can use soft beds."

"I'll find out on the payroll tonight, one way or the other," Marcus said. "Now, we simmer down. We make him and the sheriff think he's outgunned us. We just relax and enjoy all of our money for a while right here in town. In a couple of days the sheriff and everyone will relax."

"Remember, boys, we're all happy," Hank said. "Hell, each of you just earned a thousand. That's three years' pay for honest work."

Outside it was almost dark. Marcus walked back to his hotel room, washed up again, and then meandered down the street toward the alley that would lead to the schoolmistress's house. He hoped that she was home.

Marcus knocked on her back door. He waited a minute and didn't hear any movement. He knocked again and this time someone stirred inside. The door opened and Agnes peered out.

"Miss, I'm an out-of-work cowhand riding the grub line. I was wondering if you'd have a place a man could spend the night?"

She grabbed his shirtfront and pulled him inside.

She kissed his lips in the dark kitchen. "I heard you were back in town, and rich."

"Partway rich. He still owes us twenty thousand dollars."

"I heard that, too. He bought the sheriff, that's what everyone says."

"Don't make no never-mind," he said, and kissed her, pulling her tightly against him. When she came away from him she nodded.

"Come on," she said as she led him inside.

Later they lay exhausted on her bed, looking at the moonlight that filtered in through the lacy curtains. It was dark in the room. Quinn reached down into his pants for the makings and rolled a cigarette.

"Marcus, you got to smoke that in bed?" Agnes said. "I can think of better things to do with your hands." She started rubbing her breasts against his shoulder.

"Whoa, girl. I got me some business at the saloon."

"You can't leave here, I won't let you."

"I'll be back."

"Once more before you go," Agnes said, moving her hands slowly between Quinn's legs.

"I reckon it'll keep," Marcus said, putting out his smoke.

Later on, Quinn sat at the bar of a saloon at the far end of the street. It was where Carmichael's teamsters spent their off-duty time. Most of them drove supplies and equipment up to the Lost Man Mine. Once a month the top driver was picked to drive the payroll wagon.

He watched the men and soon saw the celebration. A swarthy man with a full beard and black eyebrows had been named the top driver of the month.

An hour later, Marcus followed him out of the saloon. A half-block down the street he tripped over his own feet and fell into the dust. Marcus helped him up.

Ten minutes later Marcus had supported the teamster all the way home. They talked and the man bragged about driving. Marcus found out the payroll would be going up the mountain in four days. It would leave at three A.M. to help avoid any outlaws who might try to steal it.

The driver was a talking, bragging drunk. He wouldn't even remember walking home when he sobered up the next afternoon.

THAT SAME NIGHT, Hank Proudy left the Elk Horn without finding much in the way of a good game of poker. He had just started to cross the deserted street when he saw a woman coming toward him.

She was short and a little on the heavy side. He smiled at her as she passed him, watching her dark blue dress sweep the boardwalk. Then she stopped and turned. He walked slowly up to her.

"Evening, ma'am." Hank tipped his hat. "Nice night for a stroll."

"Yes, providing one has someone to stroll with, Mr.—"

"Proudy, ma'am. Hank, to ladies as pretty as you."

"Thank you, Hank," the woman said, giggling slightly. "You may call me Marlene." She paused for a moment, looking him up and down. "You're a stranger to town?"

"Yep. I rode in with my friends a few days ago. Red Bluff's a fine town." Hank continued along the boardwalk and Marlene followed.

"You won't be staying long, I gather?"

"Just till we finish a little business, is all."

"I see. Hank, I'm not one for formality and such, so I'd like to ask you a favor."

"Anything in my power, little lady."

"Could you escort me home? My husband's away and with all the Indian goings-on and bar fights, a lady takes her chances walking alone after dark."

"I'd be honored, Marlene." Hank could see where this conversation was going and he aimed to go right along.

"You are kind. It's not far," she whispered. Hank took her arm and followed her lead.

Marlene turned them to the right and led on around the corner past the undertaker's establishment. Picking up the pace, they went straight south two blocks and turned left into a long alley. She pointed to the last house on the right.

"That's it," she said quietly.

"Seems like a lot of trouble to take to walk home," Hank offered as they approached the door of the screened-in back porch.

"That may be, Hank. But a lady in my position needs to protect her reputation from the gossips." She opened the door and proceeded to walk in, then turned around. "Lordy, I'm forgetting my manners. Would you care to come for a drink of something cool?"

"I'd be much obliged," Hank said, looking around casually.

They went through the mud room and entered the kitchen. Hank noticed she didn't light the lantern on the counter.

As Marlene busied herself with the pitcher and glass on the table, Hank moved up behind her and put his arm around her waist.

"Why, Hank! I don't know what to say. . . ."

In response, Hank spun her around and kissed her

hard on the lips. She responded hungrily. He kissed her again and she sagged against him, running her arms along his strong back.

"Follow me," she whispered as she took him by the hand and led him through the parlor, down a short hallway, into a small guest room.

She lay down on the bed and started unbuttoning her dress.

"Here, let me do that," Hank said, undoing the last few buttons and fondling her ample breasts.

"Oh, that just sets me on fire. Hmm, I don't know when I—"

Hank stopped her words with another kiss as he pulled down the rest of her dress. Nude to the waist now, Marlene grabbed his head and buried it between her breasts. She moaned as he sucked her erect nipples.

Gently, Hank began tugging the dress down. "Help me," he said softly. Marlene eagerly lifted her hips, squirming to shrug off her clothing. She stretched back, her legs spread, pelvis churning, urging him to come to her.

Still dressed, Hank lay her on her side. She worked quickly, unbuttoning his shirt and going directly to his pants. His huge erection made her gasp.

As she stroked him, he brought his hand up her bare inner thigh and watched her reaction. She closed her eyes and moaned. He ran his hand up and down her several times, until he could hear her breathing speed up.

Marlene caught his hand and pushed it hard at her crotch. He found the magic clit and worked it back and forth.

"Yes, darling, yes! That feels so good!"

She lifted her knees. "Right now, don't even take off your pants. My husband might be coming home anytime. Now and then he checks up on me. He thinks I'm dicking somebody. I haven't been. Until now, that is. Please, right now, quickly."

Hank lowered between her thighs and slid into her waiting slot. The first stroke made her climax, and he grinned at her wailing as she came again and again. When she finished, he drove in again, then watched her as she broke into a beautiful smile just for him.

"Oh, Lord, but it's been more than two years. You don't know what this means to me. Fuck me hard now and make it last as long as you can."

Hank did, and she gripped him with long-unused muscles. Three more times she climaxed before Hank did. Then they lay there panting together.

A dog barked down the street. She tensed for a moment, then shook her head.

"Again," she said.

"No rest?"

"Not for the wicked. You know that."

He stroked again as they thundered into another climax that left them both sagging with fatigue. He came away from her and sat there resting.

"Marlene, I'm home." The man's voice floated through the house and Hank jumped up and started for the window. She shook her head and pushed him into the closet. Then she lit the lamp, gathered up her clothes, and pulled on a robe from the closet. It was filled with clothes she didn't wear anymore. She took out a dress and held it up to her chest.

"Jonas. I'm in the guest room trying on some of these old dresses of mine. I really need some new dresses. When can we go to Denver so I can do some shopping?"

Sheriff Markowski came to the room and leaned against the frame. She held up a dress over the robe and looked in the mirror.

"You've got more dresses than any four women in town as it is. Damn, when you gonna be satisfied? Where are the kids?"

"They wanted to go play at the Orlandos and stay for supper. I said fine."

The sheriff stared at her where she held up a blue dress with big flowers on it. He made a bad face. "You really like that? Throw it away, I'll buy you a new one."

"Promises."

"Tomorrow, go down and buy a dress . . . or something."

"Yeah, I've got dinner on the stove. It's a good beef stew, with all the vegetables you like. Just needs heating."

"Better be. I'm gonna look at the paper." He turned and left the doorway. Marlene went over and closed the door but didn't latch it. She opened the closet door.

Hank lowered his .45. Damn, that was close, he thought. He wiped at sweat on his forehead. Marlene tugged at his sleeve.

"The window—quick, while he's still with the newspaper. It's your best chance."

Hank darted to the window, looked out, saw no one, and slid through it. He ran to the alley and then walked the long way down to the next block.

His heart gradually pumped a little slower. Christ, he thought he'd have to shoot his way out of that closet for a minute. Marlene handled it real smooth. Hank laughed and turned into the next street.

Christ, he'd never been so close to getting caught. And with the goddamn sheriff's wife! He'd almost taken a fast ride out of town, damn fast. The luck was with him. He headed back to saloon, hoping there'd be a big game.

Bob Depro found the girl he wanted in the second saloon he went into that night. She was short and blond and had the largest breasts he'd ever seen on a human being. She told him she wasn't half of what her mama had been.

Upstairs Bob caught her long blond hair and played with it. For a minute he thought the people who said he liked blondes because he was part Indian might have him figured out. He wanted to find a damn albino sometime. Redheads were good, too; so soft and pink all over. Bob wasn't sure if he liked them because he was Choctaw. He just enjoyed the feeling of a blonde spread out beneath him. He enjoyed the feeling three times that night.

Billy Joe hadn't seen a woman he liked since he'd come to town. For him a woman had to be big, six feet tall, wide and strong, and wanting him enough to come after him strong and hard. If she didn't chase him damn hard, Billy Joe couldn't get interested. It wasn't that Billy Joe was shy around women, but he plain scared some of them he knew, and the short ones figured they'd be smashed flat.

Hell, no problem. He'd wait till he found the right one. If there wasn't one in this town, maybe there'd be one in the next place they stopped. He took twenty dollars with him and settled down to a poker game at the dime table at the Elk Horn Saloon. If twenty dollars was all he had, he couldn't lose any more than that. He played only at house tables where table stakes were the rule.

That night luck was with Billy Joe. He knew he was a lousy poker player, but before midnight he had won twenty dollars. He bought everyone a beer around the table, folded up his chair, and went back to the hotel for a good night's sleep.

Loomis hadn't bothered looking for a woman. He was still remembering the softness of Small Flower, Badger Run's third wife in the Cheyenne camp.

Instead, he walked through town and into the unspoiled grasslands just outside. No plow had ever violated the land here. No ditch had been dug, no wheel of a wagon or coach had cut deep into the soil. No fence had been strung across the wide spaces.

Here was the pure world, natural, the way the whole West once was. Loomis sat cross-legged on the grass and stared up at the stars. Yes, they were closer here. He found the North Star and saw that the Big Dipper pointing stars were aimed straight at the North Star from where the nine was on his pocket watch.

That meant it was about ten in the evening. He folded his arms, lifted his head, and listened. Far off he heard a pair of coyotes calling to each other. A nighthawk cried for its mate. Nearby he could hear the scampering feet of the night-feeding field mice.

An owl flapped past him, making more noise than most birds ever did.

This was his land, his world. At least for part of him. He sighed. His features were half–white-eye, but his soul was Choctaw.

The next morning Quinn's Raiders, as usual, met at the cafe for breakfast at nine o'clock. The breakfast rush was over and the waitress enjoyed teasing them. She was short and thin, the daughter of the man who ran the place.

When she left after taking their orders, Hank pulled out a sheaf of bills and riffled through them for the benefit of those at the table.

"Four hundred and thirty-seven dollars earned by the sweat of my brow from holding the right cards at the right time," Hank said. "Poker is the name of the game. Nobody could beat me last night."

"Bet Bob didn't play cards last night," Billy Joe said.

"Fact is, we did play cards—between times."

They all laughed as Hank cupped his hands with fingers extended, as if trying to contain the big breasts. Soon their food came.

"I did some work last night while all of you were playing around," Marcus said. "That friend of ours comes in on the train in three days. Then that same friend will go on home by coach or wagon, leaving at three A.M."

"That's a good time of the day if you're an owl," Bob said, shaking his head. "Makes it easier, though."

"Damn right," Billy Joe said. "We can get ahead on the wagon trail and block it so the rig will crash before the driver can see the problem."

"We'll work on it," Marcus said. "Keep everything under control for the next three days. Don't take any chances."

Hank laughed. "Hell, Marcus, taking chances is half the fun of living."

He told them about his meeting with the sheriff's wife. They hooted and teased him the rest of the breakfast.

"Hey, I was just paying back that shit-eating sheriff for lying about the size of that reward," Hank protested.

"Damn, but you take risks just for the good of the Raiders," Marcus said, and they all laughed again.

143

THE NEXT TWO days slipped past with little of note for the Raiders. Quinn made sure that they stayed out of trouble. He watched Hank win another hundred dollars at poker and then blow it all on one throw of the dice at the crap table.

Agnes Ballard played host for Marcus for both nights and seemed to be getting used to having him around.

Twice more Hank entertained the sheriff's wife, but both times in the more secure surroundings of his locked hotel room.

All of the Raiders had been in and out of the bank twice, each time to get change for twenty-dollar bills. They noted the two tellers and the manager who sat behind the counter as well. There was one office with a closed door and the title of President on the glass, but no one saw the door open or heard anyone inside. Three men in the whole place.

Only one door, Marcus noticed as he entered the bank that Wednesday. They would have to go in and out the same door. No guard. They would go in at three minutes to three o'clock, the closing time. They would use kerchief masks and put the men all down on the floor.

That noon they got their horses and readied them for the trail. Food sacks, the blanket rolls, everything set. They would leave their horses tied up; two down one way from the bank, and three the other way.

"Slow and easy coming out of the bank," Marcus said. "It's like the banker was letting us out after closing. Done all the time. We just act casual as all hell as soon as we get to the street."

They had never hit a bank this way, but it did eliminate the problem of breaking into the place and the vault would be open.

They tied their horses to the hitching rails at about two o'clock. Each man had a cold beer and window-shopped a little, then a few minutes before three, all five of them slipped in the bank. They all wore their long brown dusters and black hats.

One man went to each teller window. The last customer left and Marcus pushed the lock on the front door.

Billy Joe and Hank turned around at the teller cages, their masks up, six-guns showing over the counter.

"Stick up!" Hank called. Loomis and Bob vaulted the high counter and grabbed the manager before he got his hand in the top drawer. They quickly tied him hand and foot and gagged him, then tied the two tellers and gagged them.

Marcus and Hank ran for the vault. Each man had a cloth sack. They cleared out the bank's paper-money trays, then the gold coins.

At the teller windows, the Depros emptied them and then helped in the vault. It took them four minutes to find every dollar in the bank.

Hank left a note scrawled in pencil on the manager's

desk, then Hank went to the front door and stepped out, closed the door, and calmly walked to his horse. A moment later Billy Joe came out. Each man carried a sack filled with money hidden under the long duster.

Marcus was the last man to come out, and he flipped the night lock so that the door would lock automatically.

He walked to his horse and mounted, made sure the money wouldn't fall out, and worked his horse down the street away from the bank.

Before the men were half a block away, someone looked in the window and saw one of the clerks who had gotten to his feet and hopped to the window and banged on it with his elbows.

"The bank's been robbed!" the man yelled. A deputy rushed up and looked inside. He pounded on the door but couldn't open it.

It was four minutes before Sheriff Markowski arrived. He looked through the window, kicked the door, then stood back and shot the lock three times with his .45. Then he managed to kick open the big door.

Sheriff Markowski talked to the manager and ran outside, looking up and down the street. Nobody could remember anyone running away from the bank or coming out and riding away hard.

The sheriff paled. The owner of the bank would not be happy.

"A posse! We've got to mount a posse and go after these robbers," he yelled at the crowd which had quickly gathered. "Remember, that was your money in there they stole!"

It was almost an hour before the sheriff had put together a posse of twenty men armed with rifles and pistols. They rode out of town and then began to circle the area, looking for a trail made by five men. At least he knew that much. None of the bank people could give him the slightest description of the men except they were all over six feet tall, all wore black hats, and were mean.

"Jesus! Eyewitnesses who don't remember a damned thing except they all wore long dusters! No damn help at all!" the sheriff bellowed at his posse. Then he turned the posse around to check the other way. There had to be some kind of trail by five horses out of town. For a moment the sheriff paled. What the hell, they could be standing around town, waiting to take the 5:35 Union Pacific train eastbound.

When Quinn's Raiders left Red Bluff, they all rode west. There were low ridges and rolling hills there, where they could be out of sight in a half hour. Each man took a different track out of town and let his horse lope along easily at about six or seven miles an hour. That way they wouldn't raise a lot of dust or leave an obvious trail.

Single horses wouldn't be the object of any search. Any posse tracker would be looking for a group of five mounts.

Marcus grinned as he rode along. Damn, they were good! No gunplay, no vendettas by furious relatives. They would rendezvous at the cabin that Slade and his gang had used. He doubted that the posse would get anywhere near that ridge, and it would only be chance if they even rode in this direction.

A much better getaway would be on the train. Hang around town until the afternoon train came through, buy a ticket, walk on board, and be gone. The sheriff would have a lot of possibilities to think over as he started his search.

Marcus wondered how much money they got from the bank. They needed ten thousand to come out even with H. Wilson Carmichael. He doubted if there was that much cash in the bank. At least Carmichael would suffer a loss. He did not sign the letter, just chided him for not maintaining a safe bank.

Quinn met Billy Joe about five miles out of town.

"Clean as corn pone chasing a hush puppy!" Billy Joe said. "Damn, but that went easy! We should do more banks like that."

"After tomorrow we're not going to have to do anything we don't want to do for a while," Marcus said. "If we got our ten thousand here and get another ten tomorrow, that'll be five thousand for each one of us."

They rode along at a canter for a half-mile, then eased up.

"What would you like to do, Billy Joe, if you could do just anything you wanted to?"

"Any damned thing in the world?"

"Damn close."

"Like to go back to Mississippi, go back home to Bay Water, put on some fancy clothes, and hire me a rig and four, and be driven around by a liveried darkie. Yeah, that would be fine. Make all them white trash look at me and say, 'Hey, ain't that old Billy Joe Higgins?' Wooooowwweeeeeee!"

They rode awhile and Billy Joe looked at Marcus.

"How 'bout you? If'n you had your druthers?"

"Whole damn world?"

"Betcha."

Marcus grinned. "First I'd like to see Paris. Go to France and see them fancy, high-stepping dance girls in Paris."

"Then what?"

"Then, I've been thinking lately about going up into Kentucky and buying a nice race-horse breeding farm. Yeah, thoroughbreds, they call them. Expensive, but beautiful and can outrun a quarter horse all hollow for a mile."

"Racing, huh? You need more than five thousand dollars to start?"

Marcus laughed. "Probably couldn't even buy a good yearling for five thousand dollars."

"Stay away from them, then, Marcus. Why, with five thousand dollars you could go back to Bay Water and live like a king."

"Don't know if I'd want to go back there, Billy Joe. The damn Yankee bluebellies own the south now." Upstart nigras holding elected office right there in Claiborne County now. Cotton ain't what it was. I don't want to go back at all." Marcus grinned. "Besides, our families got notified all official. All five of us are dead and gone, remember?"

Billy Joe screeched with laughter. "Dang, I sure as hell don't feel dead. Wonder how much of old man Carmichael's money we got away with?"

"First thing we get to the cabin we'll count the loot."

They found the cabin much like they left it. There was still a faintly sweetish-sick smell in the cabin from burned human flesh. Billy Joe grabbed the kidnapper's body and dragged him out into the woods for fifty yards and dumped him. He stared a moment at the stump of a leg where Flinch's foot and shoe had burned away completely. The pant leg was charred up to his knee.

Billy Joe also moved Slade's body from where they had left it, then the two cleaned up the place a little, brought in some firewood, and tested the bunks that had been made with poles and sawed one-by-twelves. They still held.

The other three came straggling in. Hank was the last.

"Sat on that last little rise before I had to ride into the heavier timber," Hank said. "Checked our back trail for as far as I could see, and there was nothing moving. Hell, that damn Sheriff Markowski won't have the slightest idea which direction we went."

"Bet his wife wishes she knew," Bob said with a grin.

"Damn right. She got pleasured more times in the last three days than in the last two years."

"We need to put on a lookout?" Bob asked.

"No," Marcus decided on the run. "They won't find us even if they come this direction. What we need to do is rest up a little and then get over to that wagon road that leads up the second ridge and over it into the Lost Man Gold Mine."

They pulled out their sacks and put it on the plank table. Loomis stood guard. Hank took over the counting duties. He had them sort the bills into stacks of ones, fives, tens, and twenties. There were two fifties and two hundreds. They stacked all the gold coins in piles of ten.

Hank went to work and listed figures. He did it once, covered up his total, and counted and added it all again. At last he looked up.

"Guess?" They threw whatever they had handy at him. "All right. Grand total of eight thousand, six hundred and forty dollars. That's two thousand, one hundred and sixty dollars for each of us!"

"Yahoo!" Billy Joe screeched. He at once went and built a fire and started heating up his supper.

"More than I figured," Marcus said.

They all crowded around the small stove then and started heating up cans of baked beans and one of a beef stew. They sat them right on the top of the small potbellied stove and stirred. About half of what they ate was cold before it had a chance to warm.

They ate up two loaves of fresh baked bread and emptied out Billy Joe's jar of raspberry jam.

Then Marcus told them what he had learned from the drunken teamster who would probably be driving the wagon taking the paper and silver money up to the mine.

"He told me they always take the regular road, only one wagon goes and they pick up their escort at the edge of Fort Sanders. Usually ten troopers and one sergeant."

"Easy. What about the Cheyenne?" Hank asked it.

"They never have bothered one wagon shipment. The driver said the Indians don't care about the payroll. But when they take in a train of wagons with food and clothing, gear like that, the Cheyenne are more interested. He said they have twenty troops along then."

"Lucky us," Loomis said.

"The driver said something about a pass, that once they got through a tough pass up there, they had it downhill to the mine. Figure we should work our way up there before dark and get a lay of the land."

"Which means we need to get moving," Loomis said.

They left ten minutes later. The faint track of a wagon road went between the first and second ridges through the valley below, which was why they didn't notice it before. Now they picked it up and rode quickly up the hill.

The track had been cut in places with shovels or teams and drag buckets, and then floated with a log drag from time to time. It remained in good condition.

They didn't worry about tracks, since it would probably be still too dark to see them by five or six in the morning. The sun was almost rimming the far ridge when they came to the top of the mountain. There was a pass. It had been blasted open with powder on both sides and presented an opening not more than twelve feet wide. Room enough to get a wagon through, but not much to spare.

Marcus looked at it and began to grin.

"Ever seen an easier spot to defend?" he asked as they sat in the cut. The mountain rose in jagged, rocky spires along both sides, lifting up to the top of the two ridges.

"Take a man on a horse a damn long time to get across that bunch of rocks if he couldn't go through here," Hank said.

Bob looked over the lay of the land. It was downhill from here, on into some rocks, then past them to the start of the valley and the road on this side.

"Be easy to let the wagon get through, then bottle up this spot and not let a living thing through the pass," Bob said.

"Right on the money for a betting man," Marcus said. "I'd guess these troopers will be maybe two in front and eight behind the wagon. That way we have only two men in front to deal with. Knock down the trooper's horses. That'll stop them. We put two of us here to plug up this hole, and three down the way to take over the wagon."

"We put down the troopers up there?" Billy Joe asked.

"Play it as it falls," Marcus said. "We aren't here to handhold the U.S. Cavalry. Since the teamster driver helped us so much, prefer to see him come through this alive. Hit him in the legs if you have to."

Marcus assigned Hank and Billy Joe to stopping the troopers in back of the wagon. They got together and began picking out their firing positions. One would be on each side of the roadway. They piled up rocks to give themselves good protection.

"Damn, we could call this Fort Proudy," Hank said. Billy Joe threw a rock at him.

Below, fifty yards from the pass, the wagon road continued. Above that it was little more than a rough patch of sheet rock and boulders. The wagon would go slow getting through it.

Marcus worked out how he would take the wagon, then they all dismounted and dropped into the grass under the trees at the top of the valley. Darkness came almost at once.

"No fire," Marcus said. "Try to get some sleep. I'll be on guard until midnight. Then I'll wake up Loomis. If they leave on time at three A.M., the wagon can't get here until around six sometime. Should be daylight before then."

Marcus looked around at the shadowy faces. "Anybody got any questions?"

"How many civilians on the wagon?" Bob asked.

Marcus shook his head. "Our teamster friend didn't tell me that." There were no more questions. "Get some sleep. We'll need to be sharp and ready at five-thirty."

153

∞∞∞∞∞∞∞∞∞∞∞∞∞∞∞∞∞∞∞∞∞∞∞∞ **Chapter Sixteen**

THE SUN WASN'T up yet.

Hank moved like a soft shadow to the edge of the cut through the granite and peered down the wagon road between the first and second finger ridges that led up into the Medicine Bow Mountains near Red Bluff, Wyoming.

"Not a damn thing in sight," he called to Billy Joe Higgins, who sat thirty feet away at the far side of the wagon path passing through the rocks.

Billy Joe turned and waved at the three men below. "Nothing yet," he called.

They waited.

The sun came up, a mild dew dried off the granite, and Hank sat on a rock and waited. Where were they? Had they changed the plans? No, it was near the end of the month. The mine would want to have its payroll ready for the men. He puffed on a twisted black cheroot.

A half hour later Hank stood to relieve the hardness of the rock. Far down the valley he saw the first ribbon of dust rising into the air.

"Coming," he called. "Still about two miles off. Up the hill, should take them a half hour."

The men adjusted their shooting positions. By the time the wagon came through the pass and down the other side of the slope, the surprise element would be gone. Marcus had positioned himself in the first rocks big enough to cover him. They were thirty yards down from the pass.

He put Bob Depro across the flat rock behind a jumble of the blasted-out granite slabs. Loomis was thirty yards farther down, in the first trees that grew at the head of the valley. He would be the insurance to see that no one got past them and rode down to the mine.

Hank slid around the side of the cut and looked down the wagon road. He could see them coming better now, less than a quarter of a mile down the slope, which heaved up more sharply toward the pass. The four mules were walking now, pulling the wagon with ease.

When he was certain of the number of civilians on the wagon, Hank waved at Marcus. Then he lifted his right arm four times. Three civilian guards and the driver. They probably had shotguns. Hank would let the wagon roll right past him, then use his ten-gauge on the cavalry mounts.

He and Billy Joe had worked out the order. Hank would take the first cavalryman following the wagon, Billy Joe would use his Mare's Leg on the second. If they needed to put down more to discourage the military men, they would alternate.

Hank ran back to his firing position. Chunks of rock a foot thick protected him. He would fire through a slit three inches wide. He was no more than fifteen yards from the entrance to the pass.

Now he could hear the jangle of the harness and the crack of the bullwhip. Some old bullwhackers loved their whips so much they had adapted them to driving mules. But they had to be careful not to touch the stubborn mules with the stinging leather. The sound had to do the job.

Hank had seen two Army riders out in front of the wagon as they had guessed. Danger would naturally come from the rear. Or so the cavalry thought.

He took a quick breath now as the sounds came louder and a blue-uniformed cavalry sergeant swung into the pass and through the narrow cut. The soldier stopped a moment and looked down the hill, nodded, and walked his mount carefully across the slanted, flat, smooth rock.

Another trooper came through, then the wagon itself. Hank pushed the ten-inch barrel of the scatter gun to the very edge of the hole, allowing no part of the metal to be seen. He could see the four men on the wagon; the three guards all had shotguns.

Hank let his eyes sweep to the back of the wagon. There was a ten-yard interval before the first trooper behind the rig came into view. He aimed at the broad side of the Army mount just as it came into the pass and fired one barrel.

Almost at once he heard shots from down the trail behind him. The Army mount in the pass went down and the trooper bellowed in pain. The second trooper stormed ahead, only to be blown out of his saddle by Billy Joe. There was a pause and another trooper came forward, then swung his mount around and vanished.

Hank broke open the shotgun and ejected the spent rounds, reloaded, and flipped it shut. Just as he came back to sight in on the pass, three troopers stormed into the opening. He fired once, then again, and heard Billy Joe get off two shots. The three horses and men went down in a jumble, blocking the entrance to the pass. One man crawled out from the tangle of hooves and bodies. He had a bloody arm. He looked behind, then crawled out of sight.

* * *

Marcus saw the first two troopers come through the pass and got ready. The lead cavalry sergeant had passed Marcus's position by the time the first shots thundered into the high-country silence. Marcus had his Henry repeating rifle resting over a rock and tracking the lead mule on the wagon.

When he heard the thunder of the ten-gauge, he fired. The 216-grain .44 slug slammed into the left side of the mule's head, killing it instantly. It went down at once, dragging down its harness mate, and the second team stumbled into them as traces broke and the wagon tongue twisted to one side.

The wagon jolted to a sudden stop, throwing the three shotgun guards off the boxes they sat on and flat on their sides and backs on the wagon floor.

Bob Depro chose the trooper following the wagon as his target. The man rode high in the saddle, seemed young, and when the shotgun went off behind him, the Army man already had his pistol out of its holster.

Squeezing off a shot, Depro hit the young soldier in the chest with his Henry, and then looked at the wagon as the mule went down and the team stumbled, stopping the rig.

He had levered a new round in quickly and tracked the wagon box. When the first guard lifted his shotgun over the eighteen-inch sideboard, Bob shot him through the forehead.

Loomis coolly tracked the sergeant as he rode toward him. The man was still fifty yards away when the first shotgun blast roared through the hills. The sergeant had time to twist in the saddle before the round from Loomis's Henry caught him in the side, drove through his body, ripped apart his aorta, and plunged out through the far lower stomach.

Four more shots came from near the pass, then an unreal quiet settled down over the scene. One of the mules brayed. The driver sat rock still in his seat, wondering why he wasn't dead.

Three shotguns sailed out of the low body of the wagon. They were followed by three handguns.

"Don't shoot!" somebody in the wagon bellowed.

"We're unarmed. Hell, this payroll ain't worth getting killed for."

The driver had a pistol in his holster. He held both hands high.

"Lift your hands and stand up," Marcus thundered.

Both men came up slowly, looking around.

"Out of the box and lay facedown in the road, hands over your head, feet spread wide," Marcus ordered. "You, too, driver."

The three men moved to Marcus's side of the wagon and lay on their stomachs.

"Clear up there?" Marcus called.

Hank looked out but couldn't see anyone. "Looks quiet. Five unhorsed. Three more somewhere."

Marcus held his rifle ready as he sprinted for the wagon. There were no shots. He checked cautiously over the near edge sideboard. There sat a strongbox, tied to the floor.

"Clear that area, Hank. Push them back down the valley," Marcus called. Billy Joe ran to the pass and looked out. He lifted his Henry rifle and sent four shots slamming toward the three troopers who had retreated a hundred yards. They turned and charged away downhill.

A shotgun blast roared close to Billy Joe and he turned. The trooper with one bloody arm had lifted himself up and pointed his pistol at Billy Joe's back.

Hank's double-aught buck ripped into him, blasting his head from his shoulders. The head spun to one side, away from the heap of dead horses and bodies of troopers, and rolled a dozen feet down the hill toward the wagon.

"Damn!" Billy Joe said. "Owe you a bottle."

Billy Joe stood guard at the pass while the others worked on the strongbox. They untied it and dropped it on the rocks. It didn't come open. Two locks held it. Hank ran back up and took Billy Joe's rifle and sent him back down with his Mare's Leg.

Two rounds of the big .58 caliber blasted the locks into useless twisted metal, and the lid sprang up.

Marcus pushed the top open. Stacks of greenbacks were arranged neatly. Two sacks of coins lay nearby. Marcus lifted out the greenback bundles and pushed them inside his shirt. He handed the bags of coins to Billy Joe and Bob Depro. Marcus called for Hank to come down. It was over.

They headed for where they had hidden their horses in the woods another fifty yards down the trail.

Marcus paused over the three men facedown in the dust.

"Nothing personal, you three. You tell them we didn't kill nobody who wasn't set on killing us. Stay right where you are for half an hour or one of these Henry slugs gonna cut up your hide. You hear?"

The three said they heard.

Marcus was the last one to mount up. He'd been checking the lay of the land, and he saw another pass to the west about where the third finger ridge would wind down to the Laramie River valley.

He turned that way, working up and across the rocky terrain and into the cover of the pine forest.

"Where the hell we headed?" Hank Proudy asked as he rode alongside Marcus.

"Figure we'll move along here until we can find another excuse for a pass, go across, and come back down through the Cheyenne village or maybe this side of it. Then we can camp out for a few days and let some of the clamor die down around Red Bluff."

They heard and nodded. Marcus was their leader. They could afford to camp out a few days. The five moved out through the high Wyoming landscape toward the next valley.

Hedcccccccccccccccccccccccccc **Chapter Seventeen**

CORPORAL RANDOLPH HARDING stared at the three civilians sitting in the shade of the wagon. He seethed with anger. It boiled through him so hot he could hardly sit his horse. He hated working with civilians.

"You, the driver of this rig," Harding spat. "What's your name?"

"Tarraway, Onley Tarraway."

"All right, Tarraway. I'm putting you in charge here. You cut that dead mule out of the traces and get this wagon on down to the mine. Explain to the foreman what happened. I'm sending one rider back to the fort to tell Major Abbott the story. My suggestion is that we mount a patrol to hunt down these killers and wipe them out. They killed six good cavalry men. Now they're meat for our guns."

Onley stirred and sat up. "Corporal, you might tell Mr. Carmichael, the mine owner, about what he lost as well. He's gonna want to know. Fact is, he might send out a posse himself. Got good reason to, I'd say."

"This is an Army matter, Tarraway. I wouldn't think there would be a place for any civilians."

"Reckon Mr. Carmichael will have something to say

161

about that. It was his payroll that got stole, and one of his guards kilt."

"Perhaps, but I don't have the time. I'm going to do a scouting expedition to track the five culprits. Then, when the main patrol gets here, I'll lead them to where the culprits have holed up."

"Holed up? Hell, they'll be in Rawlins before you can spit. Think they'll sit around waiting for you?"

"Yes, if they think they got away clean. That's my problem." He crinkled his brow a minute. "Tarraway, if you really think that Mr. Carmichael will want a report, why don't you ride with my trooper back to town. You can report to Carmichael while my man goes to the fort."

Harding nodded to himself, rode off thirty yards, and caught one of the riderless cavalry horses that was not wounded. He came back and handed the reins to the teamster.

"Can you ride one of these as well as drive one?"

A half hour later Tarraway and the wounded trooper, Daniels, were on their way back to the fort and Red Bluff. Daniels's arm had been skinned with the double-aught buckshot and was now bandaged. It was painful, but he could ride. Harding told him what to say to the major and made him repeat it to him. Then he whacked the horse and sent him on his way, riding with the civilian.

Corporal Harding brought the other two cavalry men up to him, and told them what they were going to do.

"First, we leave the dead where they fell. The colonel will never believe it unless he sees it. Next, the three of us are going to pick up the trail of those five killers and track them. Either of you men any good at following a trail?"

One of the men wiped his nose with the back of his sleeve and raised his hand.

"Corporal, I used to do quite a bit of tracking, running down stray steers. Got fair to middling at it."

Corporal Harding nodded. "You're Warnick, aren't you? All right, you're our tracker. Trade weapons with one of the casualties if you've a mind; then we'll head out."

One man traded his breechloader for a solid-cartridge weapon, and they mounted and rode where the two civilians said they last saw the Raiders ride away. It was in a sparsely timbered slope that headed west and upward.

Warnick picked up the tracks after a hundred yards and pointed.

"Going up this way, Corporal. I'd say they headed toward the ridgeline, and then maybe back down the other side into the valley again."

"Why, Warnick?"

The tall, thin, trooper looked at the clouds, then at the wilderness of hills and mountains and peaks to the south. "Nothing but tall places over that way. Hell, they want to find someplace where they can spend all that money. How much they get out of that payroll?"

"No idea, Warnick. Remember, we don't want to get too close to them, just stay with them so we can send a contact back to bring the colonel up the trail, if he decides to send out a patrol."

"If? Hell, Corporal Harding, you and I both know damn well he will. He ain't lost six men in six months. He don't want to let it go unpunished, especially since they is white men."

Harding nodded and stayed behind the tracker. He took a small notebook out of his pocket and began to make a map of the area. He wanted to be covered in case Major Abbott came out.

It would take three hours for the trooper to ride back to the fort, another hour to mount a patrol, and three more hours to ride back up here. Seven hours. It couldn't be more than about eight o'clock now. They had been looking forward to a big breakfast at the mine and then a leisurely ride back to the fort.

A troop could be at the cut through the mountain at three that afternoon. He would have one of the two men with him back at the cut by three o'clock with the map to lead the troop back on this trail.

A half hour later the tracks of the five topped the ridge and wound down the other side, angling toward a valley between two finger ridges.

An hour later they came to the start of a small stream in the valley.

"They stopped here, Harding," Warnick said from where he knelt down by the stream. "Watered their horses and must have been here a half hour or more. That's 'cause there are at least three stacks of horse biscuits over here."

"Maybe they stopped to eat," the corporal suggested.

Warnick shook his head. "Don't think so. No fire, no food wrappers or cans." Warnick left his horse and walked around the grassy area. He bent and snorted. "But look at this, Corporal," he said, holding up a five-dollar bill.

Corporal Harding took the bill and checked it. "Looks like good currency to me. Suppose those murdering bastards have so much cash now that they wouldn't even bend over to pick up a five-dollar bill?"

"Damn!" Warnick yelped. "That's half a month's wages for me."

The three-man cavalry detail rode again, following the plain trail left by the five robbers. The lower they went on the little valley, the fewer trees they found. If

164

the riders kept moving, they would run out of cover in another hour.

At a good stand of trees and some covering brush, Corporal Harding stopped his detail.

"Far enough," he said. "We've got a bead on them." He looked at the two men. Phil Engle was a good enough soldier, but he wasn't smart enough to make grass grow. It had to be Warnick he sent back.

"Can't be sure of the hour since my gold watch got broke. So it's time we send somebody back to the cut in the mine road. Warnick, you get nominated, since you can find your way back to us. If the major is coming, he should be at the cut before dark. I'd guess about three o'clock this afternoon.

"If he doesn't show up by dark, you sleep over and head out here to get us, first thing with daylight. I figure that he'll be stone ground mad and chomping at his bit to take on these five civilians who shot up his detail."

Warnick snorted. "So I got to ride back and then back here again. What I get for volunteering. Last time I ever do that."

"Don't bitch, Warnick. If the major comes, he'll have food and you can beg some from the troops. Now give your horse a drink and then get your ass out of here. You get there by three o'clock if you have to run that nag into the ground. Ain't all that far."

Warnick swore and rode out from the grove.

In Red Bluff, at about the same time of day, Onley Tarraway sat in the luxurious living room of H. Wilson Carmichael. He had never even met his employer, let alone talked to him, and had ridden past his big house only once.

He had told the story of the assault and robbery as he saw it unfold. His boss had walked back and forth, his hands clasped behind his back, his potbelly leading the way. Now and then he scrubbed one hand over his face.

"You say a soldier went out to the fort same time you got here?"

"Yes, sir. He was wounded and was supposed to tell about the six men getting killed."

"Yes, yes, tragic. Also gone is a lot of hard, cold cash." He turned quickly. "Come, come, we'll go down to the fort and see what the major is going to do. This town doesn't have enough good men to form a posse, but we could get some armed men from the mine."

They rode up ten minutes later to find the fort in the middle of frantic activity. They rode directly to the commandant's office and went inside without anyone challenging them.

A sergeant looked up from his desk.

"Yes, gentlemen, what can we do for you?"

"Need to see the major about the payroll robbery and his six dead troopers."

"He's busy right now. In fact, he's getting a patrol ready to chase down the robbers."

"Good, I'm here to help him." Without another word, Carmichael walked over to the major's door and pushed it open. Three officers around the desk looked up.

"Major Abbott, are you sending out some men to run down those murdering robbers?" Carmichael asked.

By then the sergeant had Carmichael by the arm.

"At ease, Sergeant. Yes, Mr. Carmichael, we certainly are. We appreciate your interest, but this is a military matter now."

"Half-military, Major. I've got over twelve thousand dollars in cash out there somewhere."

Major Abbott straightened and dropped his pencil. "Yes, that's right. Can you supply me with thirty men

166

with good rifles and plenty of ammunition?"

"Well, no, not right away."

"That's what you'll need. I'm leading a thirty-five-man company out to that point within the hour. You may accompany us, but we won't wait for you if you fall behind. Perhaps you could get some armed men from your mine to work as a backup unit with us."

"Yes, I might be able to do that. First I'll go home and change and be back here with my own arms within the hour. Don't leave without me."

"We'll leave when we're ready. Our wounded man will remain here. The mine road is plainly marked. We won't have any problem getting up to that cut. If we miss you here, we'll see you there." Major Abbott went back to the map and the lists on his desk and his talk with the two officers. Soon a captain and a lieutenant stood and hurried outside.

The time was a little after three-thirty when Major Abbott and Captain Ted Nyberg led their thirty-five-man contingent of Baker Troop into the cut through the solid granite and met trooper Greg Warnick.

Warnick saluted smartly. "Major, sir. Private Warnick reporting. Corporal Harding was the highest surviving rank. We tracked the killers for about five or six miles, then I had to get back here. I'm ready to lead you to that point if you wish."

Major Abbott hardly heard the trooper. He stared around at the carnage, the dead troopers, and horses with hungry swarms of flies buzzing around them. He shook his head and looked back at the trooper.

"Yes, Private. Let's move out at once. Lead the way." He turned to his left. "Lieutenant Branson, detail three men to haul the horses off the roadway here and get our casualties moved out of the track so we can transport them back to the base."

167

H. Wilson Carmichael moved up beside the officer. "Major, as we discussed on the way out here, I'm going down to the mine and talk to my men. I'll get what rifles we have and men to handle them and come back this way and follow you. Shouldn't be any problem. I'll be about two hours behind you. We want those bastards as much as you do."

"Nearly as much, Carmichael. All you lost was money. My command lost six brave cavalry troopers who can never be replaced."

Major Abbott turned away, signaled forward with his hand, and they rode.

There was no hesitation this time about the route. Private Warnick took shortcuts, and moved the company back to the valley between the two finger ridges in just under an hour.

Corporal Harding saluted his major and reported.

"Sir, we've made two small scouting trips out from here as we waited. We did not see anything of the outlaws. About half a mile ahead is a long open stretch of land, but we didn't see the robbers cross it."

"Thanks, Harding. I'm hereby promoting you to sergeant. Good work on following them this far. You functioned well under fire and in the follow-up."

He turned then and sent his two best trackers out on horseback to follow the hoofprints. Major Abbott established a connecting link with the scouts, and the main force came a quarter of a mile behind them.

They moved ahead slowly for an hour. They had passed the open stretch and were still on the tracks as the sun began to sink behind the far mountains.

The connecting trooper came back and talked with the major.

The word was passed. They would make camp there for the night. Fires were permitted.

Guards were posted.

Major Abbott had Sergeant Harding brought to him.

"What kind of men were these killers? Did you get a look at any of them, hear them talk?"

"I didn't, sir. But the civilians did. They only killed one of the guards. The leader of the outlaws told the wagon guards to tell anyone who wanted to hear that the robbers killed only those who tried to kill them. There were five of them, a motley crew from what the civilians said. One huge man, two dark ones who looked like they were breeds, and two others; tall, well made. They took out our men like a disciplined Army fighting unit, sir. It was well planned, the gap here an ideal place to attack and simple to defend."

"Yes, thank you, Sergeant. That's all."

Major Abbott thought about it as he stretched out in his three blankets. These outlaws fought like regular Army. Who could they be?

MARCUS QUINN AND his men were in no hurry as they worked down the pleasant stream between the finger ridges that afternoon. They stopped to water the horses, had a quick lunch at another place from food in their saddlebags, and an hour before dusk realized that the creek they followed was winding to the right and heading out into the open prairie.

"Shouldn't we be turning over to the left if'n we want to find Rawlins?" Hank asked.

" 'Pears as how," Billy Joe Higgins said. "Guess we could go back into Red Bluff, but my guess is they wouldn't be no way glad to see us."

They all laughed.

"Let's just call a halt right here and head cross-country come morning," Marcus said. "Better to camp where we got some water for the animals."

They settled down and made a small cooking fire that was shielded in a heavy stand of trees. Loomis Depro brought sticks from the bank of the stream that were white with age and had been seasoned and dried until they had almost no moisture left in them, and would make almost no smoke.

Billy Joe and Hank started up a small dice game on

a blanket, using their stacks of dollar bills. Bob settled down in his blanket and watched the small fire. Marcus tried to remember the country ahead.

It was ten minutes later that Marcus realized Loomis had slipped out of the camp on scout.

Loomis came running back to camp after dark. He pointed back up the valley from the direction they had come.

"Company," he said. "Twelve, maybe fifteen fires, no more than a mile away. I even saw one fire flickering through some trees."

They all went to look. They had to walk only two hundred yards from their camp up the side of the finger ridge.

"Be damned!" Billy Joe said. "Who in hell gonna make fifteen campfires?"

"Looks like about a company of infantry or cavalry," Marcus said. "The damn soldier boys are tracking us!"

"Damn bluebellies after us again," Hank said softly.

Marcus sighed. "Well, we can't let them catch us now, can we?"

"Fifteen fires . . . four men to a fire," Bob Depro said. "Could be sixty of them back there. Even at ten to one, that's a little heavy on the odds. Not a chance for us to take them in an open firefight."

"You're right, Bob. So it's time for the Raiders to go into a little operation of their own. Gents, I'd say we should go on a midnight walk. Remember how we hit that Yankee company down in Missouri?"

"Oh, damn, what a night that was!" Billy Joe chuckled. "Same damn plan might work."

"First we recon," Marcus said, "just like in the old days. This bunch will have guards out. We watch for the change, then we take out the guards, two or three, I'd say. After that we have four hours before they change guards again. This will be a silent go-round until we're ready to welcome them into the party. Bring your knives."

They went back to their camp and put out the fire, packed up their goods, and got their horses ready to ride out on a moment's notice. Then they all picked up their favorite death dealers and a Henry rifle and worked silently up the side of the finger ridge until they could see the Yankee camp plainly. There were twelve fires.

"Horses?" Marcus asked.

"They have them in two groups," Loomis said. "I can hear them above and below the camp. They put them out about thirty yards or so, probably in rope corrals."

"We do the horses, but first we get the guards, then, if they stacked their weapons, we'll go for all the rifles we can grab. Just like in Missouri."

They all grinned. Marcus went at the upstream guard and Hank angled for the downstream one. They agreed to wait for the guard change, then they would move in.

The guards changed at ten o'clock. Marcus lay behind a clump of brush and watched the sleepy trooper take his place on this end of the camp. The old sentry told the fresh one where he was supposed to walk, then headed for his bedroll.

Marcus let the sentry make three trips out to the end of his post and back. On the fourth circuit, Marcus came up behind him as silently as a shadow, grabbed him around the throat with his forearm to stop any scream, and then drove his six-inch knife into the man's chest.

The first stab didn't do the job, so Marcus lifted his arm and sliced the sentry's throat from side to side, and northern blood spurted into the dead night. The guard collapsed on the ground without a sound.

Shortly afterward, five shadows crept through the camp, lifting rifles and carbines, carrying them away without a sound. They lugged the eight-pound weapons three or four at a time halfway up the ridge on either side of the valley and hid them under brush and leaves so they couldn't be seen.

After they finished collecting the rifles, the five met again just outside the camp. They split up, with Marcus and Hank going upstream to the horses, the other three downstream.

The mounts were in a loose corral made of ropes. All had on halters and reins but no saddles. Gently, silently, the two men moved into the corral, gathered six horses each by the reins, cut the boundary rope, and led the horses around the camp and downstream. When they were a quarter of a mile below the camp, they each swung up on a mount, barebacked, and led them away at a faster walk, and when the land leveled out, they galloped for three miles, then let the horses scatter downstream.

The Raiders rode bareback to just below the cavalry camp, then slapped the last five mounts on the rear, sending them galloping down the valley. There had still been no outcry from the soldiers. Marcus asked if any of the Raiders had noticed where the officers were, but no one had.

They backed off on one side and charged their weapons. Marcus gave a Rebel yell, and the five cut loose with their weapons, spraying the camp, gunning down any shadow that moved. The booming roar of Hank's shotgun roused the camp at once.

"What the hell?" one Yankee soldier roared.

Hank added his Rebel yell to the shouting and firing.

Billy Joe Higgins's Mare's Leg boomed time and again. Henry repeating rifles fired one volley after another. As men in the camp first surged upward looking for their weapons, they hunkered down into the ground or behind trees to protect themselves. A few revolvers fired in anger, but the handguns were out of range.

When the boys figured they had done all the damage they could, they broke off contact, leaving as a few more pistols were fired in anger. Quinn's Raiders ran back to their camp.

The Raiders jumped on their horses and rode down the valley, spurring on any Army mounts they saw, driving them ahead along the way.

They formed a line across the narrow valley and swept the Army mounts ahead of them, pushing them seven or eight miles down the valley before the Raiders came together for a conference.

"Got to thinking what a beautiful crossfire situation that was back there," Marcus said. "We can go back along the top of those finger ridges. Come daylight they'll be confused as hell. We can lay on top of the ridge with our Henrys and as soon as it gets light we can pound them with rifle fire until they scramble back up the valley without their horses."

They checked the time by the North Star and the Big Dipper. It wasn't even midnight yet. Bob, Loomis, and Hank went up the east side of the valley and worked up and over the ridgeline, then listened for the sounds below that would pinpoint the cavalry camp.

Billy Joe and Marcus took the west ridge and did the same thing. They came to a point where they could hear the confused babble of voices below and a few screams of the wounded.

"Damn, just like Missouri," Billy Joe said. They found spots to lie down and get some sleep before dawn.

"Figure they'll be out looking for their horses before morning?" Billy Joe asked.

"Not a chance. They don't know who is out here challenging them. They lost their rifles and their horses. Some colonel or captain is going to lose some rank over this."

Both chuckled and eased into a half-sleep with their strong right hands covering Colt .45 revolvers.

Marcus woke up just as the first traces of dawn came. He nudged Billy Joe, who was awake at once. They worked up to the ridgeline and watched over it behind small bushes as the light came stronger.

When it was fully light, they saw confusion still reigned two hundred yards below in the cavalry camp. Hank said they wouldn't fire until Marcus did. Marcus figured there were thirty to thirty-five men below. They were waking up, noncoms trying to restore some order. He watched for officers but couldn't be sure who they were.

It was time. Marcus nodded at Billy Joe and they pushed their Henry rifles over the lip of the ridge and picked out targets.

"Let's do it," Marcus said, and fired. He worked the trigger guard on the Henry, bringing in a new cartridge, and fired again. Below, the troops among the trees fled in panic. Some dodged behind trees, only to realize they were being fired at from both sides. Twenty men raced upstream and escaped the thundering storm of lead from the five Henry rifles.

Each weapon carried 13 shots, which meant 65 rounds without reloading the tubular magazine under the long barrel. When that fusillade was over, the troopers left alive in the woods below were huddled in cover praying for deliverance.

There had been no return fire. Not a rifle left in the camp had been used. Marcus saw no officer attempt to rally the troops, no noncommissioned officer braved the fire to fight back. When the firing ceased, Marcus gave a long Rebel yell and, as agreed, the five men moved back down the far sides of the ridges, mounted, and rode downstream into the broad valley they had been heading for.

"We'll ride away from these bluebellies," Marcus said. "A few hours and they'll never find us again. But I'm damn sure that they will never forget us."

Major Abbott sat up from where he had dove between two trees when the rifle fire began. He swore nonstop for five minutes as he looked at what was left of his cavalry troop. Captain Nyberg ran up and dropped beside the major.

"What the hell hit us, Major?"

"Sounded like half the fucking Confederate Army. You have a casualty count?"

"Hell, no . . . No, sir. I'll get to it." He hesitated. "Sir, you realize that all of our horses and most of our rifles are gone."

"Gone?"

"They must have walked through our camp and picked up our rifles and then led the horses away before they started shooting. Hell, evidently they could have knifed every one of our men dead in their blankets if they wanted to."

"What happened to our guards?"

"Both knifed to death."

"Goddamn. Captain, we aren't leaving here until we find those rifles and get our horses back. Send a dozen men downstream to hunt for the horses. They probably drove them down the valley. Get that casualty count and let's see what we have left."

Major Abbott kicked the tree and swore again. How could something like this happen? Who had the skill, the *nerve* to do something like *this*? That Rebel yell told him a lot. They could be a unit like Quantrill's left over from the war. He'd have a lot of explaining to do up the line.

When the captain came back he had a casualty report. Eight men had been killed, two by knife, six by gunfire. Twelve men suffered gunfire wounds. Only one of those was serious. There were thirty-three rifles and carbines missing, and all of the horses had been freed.

"Goddamn!" Major Abbott said. "Send those twelve men after the horses. Tell them to catch one each and then ride down the valley, find the rest of the mounts, and drive them back this way. I don't want a single Army mount to be lost."

"Yes, sir."

When the Captain came back he reported that Lieutenant Branson was one of the dead.

Major Abbott didn't say anything for a minute. Then he nodded that he heard.

"The rifles. The bastards must have carried them away somewhere and hid them. Take the rest of the able-bodied men and put them shoulder to shoulder and start making sweeps out of camp and up the sides of the ridge. Go all the way to the top. Don't miss a square foot of ground until you find those rifles."

Just after ten o'clock that morning, H. Wilson Carmichael rode into the camp with fifteen civilians all armed with rifles and pistols. He looked around the battered camp, slid to the ground, and led his horse to the major.

"The killers who stole my money did this?"

"Yes."

"Run off your horses, too?"

"Yes, like a band of damn Indians."

"Shit. They got to pay double. We're going after them. They still moving downstream?"

"Yes, and good luck, Carmichael; you'll need it.

These outlaws aren't saddle bums. They gave Rebel yells two or three times and employed sound strategy."

Carmichael's eyes widened. "Sounds like some damn Confederate unit."

"Something like that. They're good at it. Be careful. I lost eight more last night and this morning at dawn."

Carmichael shivered. What the hell was he doing out here? he wondered. Then he scowled. Bastards still had $12,000 of his payroll.

"Don't worry," Carmichael said. "I'll bring back their corpses for you to spit on!"

⁂⁂⁂⁂⁂⁂⁂⁂⁂⁂⁂⁂⁂⁂⁂ Chapter Nineteen

QUINN'S RAIDERS RODE easily across the flat valley north. They had decided it would be easier to ride a few extra miles and go around the Medicine Bow Mountains instead of angling across them to get to Rawlins.

There was a stage road that angled northwest out of Red Bluff and north of Elk Mountain, then rolled almost due west into Rawlins.

They were ten miles into the flatlands when Loomis came back from a short scouting mission. Loomis kept track of the terrain for them and had ridden up a small rise to check the countryside.

"Can't be sure, Marcus, but I think we have someone following us. I kept seeing sun flashes coming off metal behind us."

Marcus held up his hand by habit and the team stopped. He knew Loomis wouldn't have said anything unless he was certain there was someone back there. Marcus looked around for some cover or some terrain advantage. There was little.

A mile ahead he saw a small creek that wound down out of the Medicine Bows and angled toward the Laramie River. It was a chance. The creek had brush and a few cottonwood trees along it. A good spot to hide and see what was behind them.

"Doubt if it's anything to worry about," Marcus said.

"Damn well can't be any of that bluebelly outfit," Hank said. "We cut them up bad and spooked the whole damn bunch. They won't fight worth shit for a year."

"Won't hurt to check out this bunch, whoever they are," Marcus decided.

They rode toward the woods, but after a half-mile, they branched out, with all five going in five different directions to confuse any trackers. They rode another half mile and then all came together on the far side of the stream. It was hock deep and chattering.

Marcus surveyed the cover. Two good-sized cottonwoods. Loomis went up one of them like a squirrel to be a lookout. Marcus placed the other three at ten-yard intervals along the four-foot ravine the little stream had created during a flood stage. There was room to stand in the ditch and stay out of the water. Perfect cover and firing positions.

Marcus looked up the tree.

"Anything yet, Loomis?"

"Just a few sun flashes. They might be ten miles behind us."

"Come on down and get some rest. We'll get ready. If they're looking for us we'll make it a long-range engagement with the Henrys. You boys have enough rounds?"

They sounded off the way an old Confederate sergeant had taught them.

"About forty rounds," Hank said.

"More than sixty," Billy Joe sang out.

"Thirty-five," Bob said.

"Got thirty-nine for three magazines," Loomis said from the tree.

"Should do us," Marcus said. "Don't know about you gents, but I aim to have something to eat before the killin' starts." He went to his saddlebags and took out some beef jerky and a chunk of cheese that had only a little blue mold on it.

Hank settled down with a just lit cheroot and chewed on some jerky. "Damn, this would be a good time to have a bottle of some fine burgundy," he said.

Billy Joe opened his mouth and let out a large belch. "Ain't that Cajun for 'beef'?"

They all laughed. Loomis came down from the tree and washed off his hands in the stream, then drank. He made sure his horse was tied behind some brush, where it couldn't be seen from the far side.

"We don't let them get to the water, whoever they are," Marcus said. "We'll know damn quick if they're tracking us. If we see uniforms we shoot them out of their socks. If it's a bunch of civilians, could be a posse from town, or maybe even a ragtag bunch from the mine after us. Fools want their pay back, I guess."

The Raiders roared with laughter. Everyone was in high spirits. They had just pulled off two jobs in a row and earned a handsome profit on both.

An hour later Loomis went up the cottonwood again. When he came down he chewed on some jerky, then nodded.

"They're coming our way. Got one man out front tracking. Ain't no Army bunch, no column of fours. Can't be sure, but looks like about twelve to fifteen."

"So, they're not on a buffalo hunt," Marcus said. "I'll put the first round over their heads when they're about three hundred yards out. If they stay and fight, we cut them to pieces until they run. They're in the open and we have good cover. No contest."

"Who are they?" Billy Joe asked.

"We'll let you go out and introduce yourself and ask for their engraved calling card," Hank said.

181

They all laughed, but this time there was a nervous edge to it.

"Carmichael himself has had time to come up. He might have brought some hired guns from town or the mine. Maybe even his bank manager who pissed his pants."

Marcus looked at the lay of the land again. "Hank, you have our left flank. Don't let anybody get around you. We don't wanna get surrounded. They'll try. Bob, you've got the other flank. We'll use our Henrys to keep them out there as far as possible."

He lit up a cigar himself now and puffed on it a few times.

"If they're civilians, it shouldn't take much to scare them off," Hank Proudy said. "Say we knock down three or four of them with our first shots. They're gonna be so scared and surprised, they just might turn around and ride for their skins back to Red Bluff."

Loomis went up the tree a dozen feet and glued himself to the trunk so they wouldn't see his movements.

"Still coming. Their tracker has done this before. I'd say they're about a mile away. I can count them now; sixteen all together."

"Come on down, we don't want them spotting you," Marcus said.

They waited. Each man had cleared a firing lane in front of his weapon. After the first shot they would be pinpointed by the pall of blue smoke from the black powder. No way to get around it until somebody invented a better powder that didn't smoke.

They leaned on their Henry rifles and waited.

The next time Loomis went behind the cottonwood tree he had only to stand on the far shore of the creek and look out from the trunk.

"Less than half a mile, Marcus. They stopped to look at the brush over here."

"Eight hundred yards," Marcus said. "Too damn far. They'll come closer. We wait."

Marcus stood behind a heavily leafed bush and could see the trackers. They were too far away to recognize anyone, but they weren't Army, that was plain. As he watched, they spread out like a cavalry front formation and began moving toward the brush.

"Looks like they think we might be here, or else they don't take chances," Marcus said. "Let's not all shoot at the same man. Work the part of the line in front of you. Start firing on my second shot. First one goes over their heads as a warning. We've got another four hundred yards to wait. Let's let them come up to a hundred yards before we fire."

When the ragged line of sixteen riders came to the one-hundred-yard mark, Marcus nodded. "All right, sight in. Let's have a party." He fired over the heads of the center men in the line. They jolted to a stop. One lifted his rifle and fired.

Marcus lowered his sights to a horseman and fired. One of the men near the middle of the line slammed off his mount with a .45 round in his shoulder. The other four Raiders fired a heartbeat after Marcus.

Then it was a stuttering sound of Henry rifles discharging as the five men shot quickly, levering in new rounds, aiming, firing, levering in another new round.

They started getting some return fire now, but six of the men in the line were down, and two had turned off the far end and ridden toward the rear, hell-bent for breakfast.

Marcus checked the whole field when he had fired eight shots. Half the men were unhorsed. Four more had turned and ridden like crazy away from the slaughter. None of the men rode forward. One turned around and around on his horse, not knowing where to go.

"Cease fire!" Marcus bellowed. The guns went silent. One more round came from the civilians in front, then a deadly quiet settled over the field. Two more riders broke from the bloody scene and raced to the rear.

One man on the ground struggled to get on a horse. He had blood on his shoulder. At last he made it and leaned over the horse's neck as he rode away.

"Damn you Rebels!" a voice came at them. The man evidently was too hurt to get on his horse.

"Anybody hit?" Marcus called.

"Got a little crease in my arm," Hank said. "Just a scratch."

"Loomis, look at it," Marcus ordered.

Loomis ran down to where Hank leaned against the bank.

"Damn big scratch," Loomis said. "Round went through Hank's upper arm. Missed the bone. He won't use that wing for a week or two."

Loomis wrapped up the bloody sleeve, putting a compress over both the red-splashed bullet marks. Then he made a sling from Hank's neckerchief.

Marcus watched the battlefield. Two men moved. Half a dozen horses stood around. Seven bodies lay in the field, either dead or too wounded to move.

"Let's get out of here," Marcus said. "Haul our asses on down the road. Those troops won't bother us anymore."

Two hours later they were well out in the broad valley that stretched twenty miles to Red Bluff and beyond to the east. They continued on their northwest route.

The letdown after the battle was over and the men talked about what they would do in Rawlins when they got there.

"Guess we missed that Cheyenne village," Billy Joe said. "I figured Loomis would want to cuddle up with a few of them Cheyenne squaws. Must be a lot of unhappy wives in Hawk's Eye's camp."

"Billy Joe, I got to tell you again, all cats are gray in the dark," Loomis said.

Before he finished the sentence, all five of the Raiders were shouting the words with him. They all belly-laughed as they rode.

Soon they came to another wandering creek, and Marcus pulled them up to it to water the horses.

"We counted the payroll money yet?" Loomis asked.

"We ain't counted it!" Billy Joe yelped.

They took the money out of saddlebags, and Hank spread out his duster on the ground and he counted the loot. The paper money was all banded and had figures written on the outside. The coins took longer, but soon Hank had a figure.

"Twelve thousand, four hundred and eighty-nine dollars," Marcus said. "Damn, there is justice, after all. H. Wilson Carmichael promised us twenty-five thousand to bring back his little girl. At last he paid it, even though he didn't want to or plan to or figure he'd have to."

Bob Depro snorted. "Yeah, we made an honest man out of him. Now maybe in Rawlins we can find some dishonest women."

They looked at each other and broke out laughing.

They put the money away. There was plenty of time to divide it later. Now they all gave a hoot and a shout and rode toward the stage road they could see in the distance. They were eager to get on to Rawlins and see what that town held.